THE WAR HERO'S LOCKED-AWAY HEART

BY
LOUISA GEORGE

First published in Great Britain 2012
by Mills & Boon, an imprint of Harlequin (UK) Limited.
Harlequin (UK) Limited, Eton House,
18-24 Paradise Road, Richmond, Surrey TW9 1SR

© Louisa George 2012

ISBN: 978 0 263 89209 3

Harlequin (UK) policy is to use papers that are natural, renewable and recyclable products and made from wood grown in sustainable forests. The logging and manufacturing process conform to the legal environmental regulations of the country of origin.

Printed and bound in Spain
by Blackprint CPI, Barcelona

they were
But in the n
e held him stea

Dear Reader

People often ask where I get inspiration from. For me, my stories begin with a single image rattling around my head. For my first book, ONE MONTH TO BECOME A MUM, it was a car crash scene. For my second book, WAKING UP WITH HIS RUNAWAY BRIDE, it was a woman painting over a stain on a wall. For this story it was the image of a lone man standing on a jagged outcrop staring out to sea. From there I ask myself lots of questions: What event has led up to this moment? Who is he? What does he want? What does he fear? The answers to these questions form the backstory and the plot usually takes care of my characters and the plot usually takes care of my

Adam, the man on the outcrop, was a gift of a hero for me to write: scarred and broody with a frozen heart. He fought hard, determined not to fall in love at all—and definitely not with a woman who'd help him leave the place that had begun to help him in

Skye first appeared as a minor character in WAKING UP WITH HIS RUNAWAY BRIDE, but this soon made it clear that she wanted her own story and felt she deserved it. If only she'd known what I had in store for her!

Beautiful Atanga Bay, with its white sand, dramatic dark crags and stunning waterfall, is the perfect place to fall in love. But both Skye and Adam have personal demons to conquer before they can come to even believe in a happy-ever-after. With the clock ticking and both denying their attraction they have a rocky road ahead of them.

I hope you enjoy reading Skye and Adam's story, in the Medical Romance™! I love to hear from readers, so please visit me at www.louisageorge.com

Warmest wishes

Louisa George x

A lifelong reader of most genres, **Louisa George** discovered romance novels later than most, but immediately fell in love with the intensity of emotion, the high drama and the family focus of Mills & Boon® Medical Romance™.

With a Bachelor's Degree in Communication, and a nursing qualification under her belt, writing Medical Romance seemed a natural progression, and the perfect combination of her two interests. And making things up is a great way to spend the day!

An English ex-pat, Louisa now lives north of Auckland, New Zealand, with her husband, two teenage sons and two male cats. Writing romance is her opportunity to covertly inject a hefty dose of pink into her heavily testosterone-dominated household. When she's not writing or researching Louisa loves to spend time with her family and friends, enjoys travelling, and adores great food. She's also hopelessly addicted to Zumba®.

Recent titles by this author:

WAKING UP WITH HIS RUNAWAY BRIDE
ONE MONTH TO BECOME A MUM

**Also available in eBook format
from www.millsandboon.co.uk**

**Praise for
Louisa George:**

'A most excellent debut from Louisa George.'
—*www.GoodReads.com* on
ONE MONTH TO BECOME A MUM

With special thanks to:

Nigel and Gina, Mel and Mel, Nicki and Shaun, Simon
and Christine, Gaynor and David. For your support
and the laughs and your enduring friendship.

Nas Dean—promoter extraordinaire!
For navigating me through the jungle that is
a virtual blog tour! You're amazing!

This book is dedicated to my boys:
Warren, Sam and James.

Thank you for supporting me, loving me
and making me smile every day.

I love you.

CHAPTER ONE

'Four. More. Weeks. Four. More…'

Skye Williams repeated her mantra with every muscle-screaming step on the last five hundred metres of her beach run. In four weeks she would hit Europe a dress size smaller if it killed her. And judging by her raging heart rate and throbbing joints, it probably would. She hated running, but it was a necessary evil.

As she dug deep for the home stretch a westerly wind whipped hot sand across her face with a ferocity that bordered on microdermabrasion. She brushed a hand across her stinging cheek. *At least I won't need that facial now. More dollars for the travel fund.* 'London. Paris. Athens. Rome.'

The thought of her newly bought plane ticket spurred her on. Freedom. A new beginning. Finally. After too many false starts.

By the time she reached Atanga Bay she'd almost doubled over, hauling in every blessed lungful of oxygen she could. Stretching out her hamstrings, she glanced over to the rocks and the ocean beyond, waiting for the endorphin rush to kick in.

It didn't.

Instead a mix of frustration and inquisitiveness piqued her.

He was there again.

The stranger. Staring out across the roiling water, standing tall against the horizontal wind. Hands stuffed into jacket pockets, immovable on the outcrop of jagged rock.

A stranger with a death wish.

Yesterday she'd left him to his fate, but evening westerlies brought huge freak waves. The all-too-familiar tug of responsibility fired her into action. Responsibility—her byword. The weight of it had dragged her down too much, too young. Too soon. She'd had enough to last her a lifetime.

And yet she still couldn't resist.

'Hey. You. Yes…you. Excuse me… Hey!' She tried to make her voice reach him through the wind as she forced her aching muscles to work. She strode closer. Not too close. The waves had doubled in size in the time she'd been out for her run. 'Those rocks are treacherous. You need to get down. It's not safe.'

The stranger turned slowly to face her, as a wave battered the rocks at his feet, his face made up of shadows and half-light. 'You talking to me?'

His voice, deep and soft—sad almost—curled something in Skye's gut. It threw her off centre. She frowned, and refocused. This wasn't the time for thinking about sad voices, she'd had enough of her own.

She suffused it with urgency. 'It's dangerous. Didn't you read the sign? Please, be careful.'

There she was, sounding like the mother hen she'd become. At twenty-eight with no kids of her own, but with honours in mothering skills.

'And why should you care?'

'I don't. I'm just trying to help. The waves can knock you off balance. I either holler at you now, or I call Search and Rescue out to look for you in an hour. They're busy people. They have lives.' He didn't look as if anything would budge him. Not least her flimsy voice, whipped half-away in the battering gale, or her appeal to his better judgement.

But the stranger stepped across the rocks, jumped down the last three feet and thudded onto the hard sand. Not so much next to as above her. She scanned up his body until her neck almost hurt.

God, he was tall, with wide shoulders strung back in an at-ease stance. His chestnut hair stood up in tufts, buffeted by the wind. A craggy scar sliced his cheek, like a cleft in a cliffside. He had a man's face, not pretty but real, handsome. Close up what remained of those shadows now edged his startlingly blue eyes. 'Do you force advice on everyone, or just people you don't know?'

'Pretty much anyone who'll listen. I'm well practised, I have three younger brothers. You looked like a willing victim.' She countered his gruffness with a smile. Dragging three boys up had taught her that meeting rudeness with rudeness never brought about harmony. And being overly cheerful usually took them by surprise, knocked the corners off their mood.

She hoped it might work with Mr Charmless here, then she could go home with a clear conscience. One more needless accident prevented. 'Seriously, I'm trying to help. You're safer on the pier. There's a sign, over there. It says—'

'I know what it says. Keep away from the rocks. Yeah. Yeah.' He stuck his hands back into his pockets again. He might as well have had his own sign up flashing, *Keep away.*

Good idea. Drop cheerful. Adopt aloof. 'I should mind my own business. Sorry. But I haven't seen you before and we prefer to keep our visitors alive around here.' What she really needed was to shut up and go home, but now she was stuck in a conversation with a hunk of grumpy man. She was dripping with sweat, her thighs red from chafing. And blathering. Could it get any worse? 'I thought you might be at risk.'

'Of what exactly? Death by nagging?'

Grumpy? Scratch that. Try downright obnoxious. Though he probably had a point.

Skye ran a hand over the spikes she'd so carefully arranged that morning, imagining how she must look. Dishevelled. At a push, in her imagination, interestingly windswept. In reality, wind battered. Her mascara and kohl had no doubt run down her cheeks. Clownish. Or like a panda. Worse? Oh, yes. And decidedly uninteresting.

She shrugged. Interesting didn't matter. Especially not interestingly rude. She'd had enough of rude men to last her a lifetime. She'd bet anything that French men weren't rude. Or Italians. Or Greeks.

Four more weeks until she found out. In person.

But this guy—this red-blooded down-to-earth Kiwi bloke—he was beyond rude. Oh, yes. She couldn't help but thrust out her chin. 'Hey, don't mind me. I'm only trying to save your life here. No big deal. And a thank-you wouldn't go amiss.'

'Save it for someone who needs it.' He looked back to a black dot way out in the ocean, lost in thought. Then his back snapped ramrod straight. 'Like him.'

Grabbing her by the hand he pulled her to the water's edge. 'See him. There? Out way beyond the break?' He pointed to the black dot. To the untrained eye it might have been a seal, flotsam in the unforgiving waves. But this was a popular place for surfers. Probably one of the locals. Skye's heart slammed in her chest as she swivelled to peer at the surf rescue clubhouse. Empty.

The stranger peeled off his jacket, kicked off his boots. 'He's waving. He's in trouble. Be my spotter?'

'Spotter? Are you sure? Are you mad? It's all kinds of crazy out there. Can you even swim?'

'Quit worrying. I've done this before. Many times.' He turned her to face him. His hands firm on her shoulders, his eyes ardent with action. His voice back to soft. But he was totally in command, clearly used to giving orders, and having them followed. 'Don't panic. The last thing I need is a hysterical woman to deal with as well. Do exactly as I say.'

Her hackles rose. As an experienced nurse she prided herself on her calm handling of any situation. 'I'm not—'

'I need you to watch him, to know exactly where he is at all times. And if I look over to you, you must point him out. The sea's rough today and it gets disorientating.' His eyes bore into her. 'Okay?'

'But…? Back-up?' The first rule of emergency, get help.

His flattened palm indicated the empty cove. 'On a deserted beach? You are back-up, lady. Call for help if you have a mobile phone somewhere in those shorts. Which looks unlikely.' He threw her a phone. 'Or use this. But stay here.'

And with that he inched his jeans down well-toned legs, revealing tight black boxers and another jagged scar that stretched from left knee to ankle. His blue T-shirt hit the ground in front of her. Skye drew her eyes away from his feet to a small tattoo on the tight plane of his tanned chest. Right over his heart.

Then he was gone, his taut, muscular body thrashing through the churning water like a demon. And she stood gaping like a wet fish, stunned at the speed in which he'd simultaneously entranced and shocked her. Wondering why, when she had very definite plans to hot-foot it out of Atanga Bay at the earliest opportunity, she wanted to see that tattoo again. Close up.

Not on my watch. Not again. A mouthful of Hauraki Gulf salt water ran down the back of Adam's throat as he fought the waves to get to the surfer. He kept his heart rate in check. Used the adrenalin shunting through his veins to fuel actions, not hinder them. Focused his thoughts on saving. Not losing.

Semper agens—Semper quietus. Always alert. Always calm. The medical corps motto beat a regular rhythm to every armstroke. Fifteen years of service and the rhythm spurred every action, like a heartbeat, a breath. A tattoo engraved on the sinews in his heart.

An elevation. A funeral dirge.

Years of hard army training, honing his body to a rock, moulding his mind to not accept defeat, had brought him to this. Water battered over his head, blurring his vision, testing his nerve. Defeat? He pushed that thought away. The drowning guy needed him. And right now he was the only hope of saving him.

Thick, heavy waves dragged him back, just out of reach of the surfer, whose hand now flailed along the top of the water instead of waving. Amazing how exhaustion could rip through a man battling nature in a matter of minutes.

Adam kicked closer. Pain squeezed his leg like a vice. The cold water gripped the ragged scarring. *Don't give in.* He pushed all thoughts of pain away. Then lost sight of the man.

Damn. Drawing on all his strength, he trod water, got his bearings. Glanced to the shoreline, where that strange woman paced and pointed. Damned cheeky but cute. In a weird kind of way. He imagined the deep espresso colour of her eyes, the crazy half-spiked hair. The intriguing tiny jewel in her nose. Ample curves. Interesting curves.

So not what he needed to be thinking of right now. Or ever.

She gesticulated, and he followed the line of her arm to the surfer. He gave her the okay signal.

First time he'd given any woman a second thought since Monica. And here he was in the middle of a rescue operation, neck deep in freezing water. Exactly how he'd felt when they'd ended their fated marriage.

There's a lesson there.

Focus on the task. 'Hey, mate! Mate! Over here.'

He got the attention of the guy, who feebly raised his head. Adam saw a huge red gash across his pale forehead. Shark meat too. Great. 'I'm coming for you. Hold on.'

The lad nodded, then disappeared under a ferocious wave. A few metres away. Metres. Nothing. *You can do this.*

Adam sucked in air then duck-dived under the current, grabbed for an arm, a limb, some piece of the man. When his hand knocked against something soft he grabbed and kicked to the surface. Bingo.

'Hold on. I've got you.' He tossed the struggling surfer over onto his back, gripped him under his shoulders and kicked towards shore. 'Stop fighting me. It's all good now. We're okay.'

The woman, her smile broad like a beacon, ran waist deep into the water and helped drag the surfer to solid ground. Which was just as well, because as Adam met her large kohl-rimmed eyes again the earth seemed to tilt. Just a little.

Or maybe it was the shock of the cold air, the shifting of the sand. His leg pinching again. 'Give me a hand to lay him down. He's breathing, but he swallowed a good part of that ocean.'

Before he could give her more instruction, she'd flipped the surfer onto his side and was kneeling at his face, assessing the wound like a pro. 'Hey, Lukas. Lukas?'

Slowly their patient focused on her, then coughed. 'What…?'

'It's Skye. It's okay. You're safe now. You okay? Took a good dunking, eh?'

Sky? Adam frowned. What kind of name was that? Curious, too, that it was the one thing that spooked him. Sky. Open air. Nothing but a long way down to a hard landing. And pain. He shuddered.

Sky. For a name? But it went with the territory. Unconventional. Unpredictable. And right now shivering in a flimsy black sports top and matching running shorts. Sea water had slicked her clothes to her body. *Fascinating.*

He bent down to help her assess the surfer. Not that she looked like she needed help. She was calm and focused. Unlike him. She was distracting. He was distracted.

In every rescue mission he'd ever undertaken he'd never allowed himself to be distracted. Never. 'Okay, Lukas. Let's have a good look at you. Got a whack from the board?'

'Yeah.'

'Nasty business.' She smiled again at the surfer. Seemed she had enough smiles for everyone, and a few to spare.

But she looked like she really cared for Lukas, like she wanted him to feel better. Like she wished she could take away his pain. Unlike his own automaton reactions. He knew how to follow strict army orders. First priority: action. No time for emotion. But she managed to mix the two with great effect.

She peered into the boy's face, got him to focus on

her. 'Great surf today, though. Bet you caught a few good ones, eh?'

Lukas nodded and managed a weak smile. 'Awesome. But I lost the board. I think it smashed on the rocks.'

'Never mind, better the board than you. Sean says the change of seasons is the best time to surf. Something about the moon or the equinox. Makes no sense to me.' Her bubbly chattering seemed to put the lad at ease.

As she spoke she ran confident, slim fingers across his forehead, probing the wound and feeling for damage. Obviously trained in medical examination and filled with genuine concern. Not the kooky, useless type he'd pegged her as. Served him right to make huge assumptions based on his past experience with women.

'How you manage it I don't know. I tried it once and ended up face-planting in the shallows. I had sand burn for weeks. Never again. But you make it look so easy.'

Fleetingly, as he watched her fuss around Lukas, Adam felt a keen sense of loss on what he was missing out on. Human contact. Warmth. Sharing things. It had been so long since a woman had given him the slightest fuss he wondered if it was time to start dating again.

Then he cast that ridiculous notion aside. One messed-up marriage was enough.

No, he was looking for simplicity. Just him and nature. Settled in serene Atanga Bay. Well, that's what he'd heard anyway. Near drownings excepted.

She continued with her gentle chatting. 'I've phoned for an ambulance, Lukas. But you know what it's like, it could take time.' She turned to Adam, fixed him with those striking dark eyes. The short black hair intrigued him. So unlike the willowy blondes he usually dated. *Had* dated. 'They're always overworked and short-staffed, I'm afraid.'

'Same story wherever you go.' But not short-staffed any

more. He opened his mouth to contradict her. Thought better of it. It would take too long, and he didn't want to get embroiled in a conversation. And, heck, what did it matter? He hadn't shared an iota about himself with anyone for years. Why would he start with her?

And yet her smiling eyes stirred something in him. Something which would be better left well alone.

'You holding up, mate?' He looked at Lukas. Did a mental check as he tried to do a blood sweep through the surfer's wetsuit. Bit difficult with a second skin. Still, it'd work as a pressure aid while they sorted him out.

'I'll just check your vitals again.' Skye took a quick pulse rate. He'd only known her two minutes and they were working in pure harmony, an understanding of the essentials hovering between them. Not just distracting, but unsettling too. 'Your heart's pumping a bit quicker than I'd like, but I reckon you'll live.' She squeezed the guy's hand. 'We just need to get that head to stop bleeding.'

Adam curled his T-shirt into a knot and held it against the wound to stem the blood flow. 'Sorry about this, mate. It was clean on this morning, I promise.' That mustered a weak smile from his patient. 'You're going to need a few stitches in that head. Any pain anywhere else?'

Lukas twisted to sit up and held out his right hand. 'My arm hurts.'

'Let's take a look.' Adam helped peel the wetsuit to waist level, scanning Lukas's body for any signs of damage or internal bleeding. Then examined his arm, aware that Sky had put herself between Lukas and the ripping wind. She looked more bedraggled than a puppy at bathtime, with those accentuated huge eyes. She was covered in damp sand and her clothes were dripping wet, her arms blue with cold.

He threw her his jacket and she wrapped it round their

patient's shoulders. 'Sky? It's starting to get dark and if we're not careful we'll all have hypothermia too.' Not a great start to day one of the rest of his life.

She shivered, but smiled. Again. Didn't her mouth hurt with all that grinning? Then she rubbed her hands up and down Lukas's shoulders. 'He's right. We don't want you to get too cold, or go into shock. You need to get warm.'

Patient first. Was she a nurse? A doctor? A local?

Did she live here? His mouth dried.

Stupid. Of course she did, hence the nagging about the rocks. If she was medical their paths were bound to cross. He shook his head, tried to clear his waterlogged brain. She was trained and skilled and here. That was all he needed to know. Any more was unnecessary detail.

A few minutes in her company had proven her curves, her weird charm and her megawatt smile were bad for his equilibrium. Four years on from a broken marriage, a broken life, and he'd only just got his equilibrium back. So he would muster polite. Nothing more.

He felt along Lukas's arm, noticed the bruising and swelling, the wincing as he touched the forearm. 'Pain here? What about here? It's swollen. Could be a fracture, hard to tell with the naked eye. You'll need an X-ray—'

A siren cut him off. He followed Sky's gaze to the main road and watched with relief as an ambulance drove down the small boat ramp. He hauled on his jeans and helped Lukas to stand.

Within minutes they'd handed over and lifted their patient into the back of the van. As he shook hands with the ambulance officer Adam decided to come clean. It would be strange turning up to work on Monday morning knowing they'd all shared this rescue and them not knowing his identity.

If he was going to settle here—and he *was* going to

settle this time—he'd need to give more of himself than name and rank. Truth was, opening up after everything that had happened often proved hard.

He spoke to the AO first. 'I guess you should know, I'm Adam. Adam Miller. Paramedic. I start on Monday, at Wellsford base.'

'Hi, Adam. Thought there was a look of expertise to this job. What a welcome, eh?'

'Lucky I was here. Just one of those things.'

'There I was thinking I was dealing with an average Joe and all the time you're a medic in disguise.' Sky blinked up at him. 'Are you going to live here, or closer to the base in town? Have you got a family here too?'

He turned his surprise at her inquisition into a cough. He'd forgotten how small-towners liked to chat. In retrospect maybe moving to Auckland would have been a better choice. He could have lost himself in the anonymity of crowds. 'I'm renting up the road.'

'We're very pleased to have you.' Dan, the AO, shook his hand. 'Kick back a bit and get out of the rat race? Atanga Bay's usually pretty quiet, but the towns round about keep us busy. Now they've extended that motorway we get our fair share of MVAs.'

Adam helped Dan close the van doors. 'Judging by the hairpin bends, I'm not surprised.'

'You're ex-army, is that right? No wonder you made mincemeat out of those waves. Quite the hero.'

'I don't think so.' *Hero? No chance.* Adam swallowed back his usual dismissive retort and the memories of his last day in action. He forced himself to be friendly. It had been so long he'd almost forgotten how. 'Before I joined up I was a surf lifeguard. I just follow my instincts.' He caught Sky's glance and remembered the importance of a positive debrief. 'And Sky was great too.'

'Our Skye *is* great. And we're all going to miss her.' The AO winked at the shivering woman and wrapped an arm round her shoulders. 'How long to go now?'

She peered up at him, her fists all screwed up like a kid's at Christmas. Her lips were slightly parted, her mouth soft. A wave of something unfamiliar washed over Adam. He ignored it. Put it down to adrenalin.

'Four weeks, three hours and...' She glanced at her watch, and laughed. A light, unencumbered sound, something he hadn't heard much, or done himself, in a very long time. 'Thirty-two minutes. Not that I'm counting. Much.'

'And then?' Adam asked, despite his misgivings at having a conversation with her.

'Then I live my life. This is just a rehearsal.' More smiles. This time they were backlit with blatant excitement. 'I'm going on a tour, travelling through Asia to Europe. To see the sights, the food, the people. Then I'm going to hit London. It's all I've ever wanted to do. I can't wait. I'm so excited.'

'So I see.' A shot of relief mixed with a sense of something ending before it had begun mixed in his gut. 'But is Europe ready for all that enthusiasm?'

Her eyes darted across to him in question, for the first time since he'd met her, she frowned. He ducked his gaze away.

See? Exactly why he shouldn't attempt a normal conversation with her. He was so out of practice he'd made her excitement fizzle. Better to just keep quiet and wait until he could get the heck away.

Dan squeezed Skye in under his shoulder, like a kid sister or a pet. 'We've been trying to convince her to stay, but she's adamant she wants out of here. God knows why. Atanga Bay has everything you could ever want. A decent chippy. A fine pub. Old friends. She's mad. What has Paris got that we haven't?'

'Style. History. French accents.' She shrugged her shoulder in a Gallic gesture. *'Pain au chocolat.'*

'Pah! Pollution. Too many people. And no ocean.' Dan eased away from Skye, climbed into the van and gunned the engine. 'Well, Adam, good to have you on board. It'll be a pleasure having you around.'

A pleasure? Skye didn't think so. Adam was rude and disturbing. And that ruggedness just deepened and deepened. But, with little regard for his own life, he'd saved Lukas so for that she should be grateful. 'Thanks for everything you did out there. By the way, we'll probably bump into each other over the next few weeks until I'm gone. I'm the practice nurse at the surgery here. Skye Williams. That's Skye with an "e". I'm named after an island, in Scotland.'

'With an "e".' He huffed out a breath and scuffed his bare toes into the cold sand. 'That makes a world of difference.'

'Sorry?'

'Nothing.' He stuck out his hand. 'I should thank you for your help with Lukas.'

Don't force yourself.

'No worries. Civil duty and all that.' She doubted he knew what civil was.

Just to show him she could rise above his rudeness she put her hand into his and shook it, trying to ignore the shot of electricity that tickled up her arm at his touch. Her eyes found his and there was a sudden connection there, a fleeting warmth she hadn't seen before. A shy heat that rebounded and hit her cheeks.

She realised that the rest of her was shivering. She looked down at her sand-covered legs and the goose-bumps along her arms. And felt the heat of his eyes over her body as he followed her gaze. It had been a long time since she'd felt that kind of warmth, uncurling something in her gut, spreading through her abdomen.

Then when she locked eyes with him again the guarded shadows had returned.

She was used to her brothers, who wore their pubescent hearts on their sleeves, whose every emotion she could read like it was her own. She'd learnt pretty quickly to understand exactly what her stepdad had thought too, even before he'd thought it himself, just so she could avoid the inevitable.

But reading Adam Miller? It was like he had so much going on behind those eyes but fought frantically to keep it all sealed away. At least, he clearly wasn't interested in sharing it with her.

Good idea. He's grumpy and bad-mannered and way too attractive for your own good.

It was time to go home. She didn't want to feel stirrings of anything. Not lust or desire. Or anything that would lead to hurt all over again. She didn't have the time or the energy. She had to focus on sorting out her life and finalising her travel plans. She dropped his hand, letting the heat evaporate. 'I should go.'

'Yes.' Without so much as a goodbye he walked towards the car park, his boots hanging from one hand. She noticed a slight favouring to the left. A barely perceptible limp, and she remembered the scarring. It didn't detract from him, no. Not at all. The way he carried himself, erect and proud, the way he hid his limp like a secret, intrigued her. Compelled her to watch him again.

'Oh, and next time you'd better keep your clothes on!'

Duh. The words were out before she had a chance to stop herself. One day she'd learn to keep her mouth shut.

He turned slowly and leaned against his truck, confusion and—was that incredulity?—on his face. She got the distinct impression that *smile* wasn't in his vocabulary. Whereas dark, brooding and mysterious took centre stage. 'Sorry?'

Yes, she was. For saying anything, and now she had to follow through. 'Or you'll get a reputation.' She waved, trying to cover her cringing with a smile.

Before she said anything else equally as embarrassing she clicked her brain back to mothering mode and mentally checked off her evening to-do list—dinner, washing, laundry. Then the luxury of adventure-planning—visas, itinerary and packing. Nowhere in there was space for *focus on grumpy mysterious strangers with abs to die for.*

She watched Adam take off his jacket, revealing his bare torso again, and the tiny tattoo—a black and yellow dragonfly, she'd discovered—before climbing into his dusty truck. And she had the strangest feeling she needed to keep well away from Adam Miller's tortured body, naked or not.

CHAPTER TWO

THREE days into the job and Adam had started to get twitchy. The view of the inside of the ambulance station was getting old. He eased the muscles in his shoulders, stretched his arms out and cracked his knuckles. 'At what point do I actually get on the road and do something?'

'Today's your lucky day.' Dan opened the ambulance cab door and climbed in. 'The paperwork's over, and your induction complete. Once we've finished the checks we're good to go.'

'Great. Bring it on.' Adam exhaled deeply, finished his supply checks and stared at the cab radio, willing it to spring into life. Not that he was itching to get his hands on sick people, more that he needed something to keep his mind occupied. It had been too long since he'd done anything useful. Four long years in a jittery guilt-fuelled wilderness. Until he'd realised that feeling sorry for himself didn't honour the memory of the people he'd lost. That action eased the pain of survival.

And being busy would keep his mind off dark, steamy eyes and tantalising curves. Starting the job for real would focus him on his true intent: getting on with the rest of his life. At least he could. There were others less lucky. He owed those not here any more a grab at a decent life, when theirs had been ripped away.

'Here we go.' Dan flicked the receiver as a crackly call came through. 'Your wish is my command.' He waited until Adam belted in then started the vehicle. 'Eighty-four-year-old female with shortness of breath. We're about twenty minutes away.'

'Twenty minutes for an SOB?' Adam bit back a surge of frustration. 'How sick is she going to be when we finally reach her?'

'Most of our time is spent getting to and from the patients and then to and from the hospital. The first responder gets there first, if they're available, and gives us a call if we're needed. That's country medicine for you. We do the best we can. Anything too serious gets choppered to Auckland. Hold on.' Dan revved up the engine and pulled away from the ambulance station.

Adam nodded. 'This is going to take a bit of getting used to.'

'Hardly front-line stuff here. Hope you don't find it too slow?'

'I'm looking for slow. Slow's good.' There had been times when he wouldn't have cared. Slow. Fast. Live. Die. But he'd dragged himself back from that bleak darkness and was determined to leave the past alone. Slow seemed a pretty good start. Slow meant he could take in his surroundings, appreciate the beauty of now. Try to live in the moment. 'I needed a change of scenery. Driving around this countryside is good for my soul.'

'You've got to admit it's a cool place to live.' Dan pointed to the undulating, bush-clad hills and the deep turquoise ocean as they passed yet another secluded deserted cove. 'Such awesome views. It's a tough job, but someone's got to do it. Must make a change to the army?'

'Yeah.' Adam chewed his cheek as his gut kicked. As soon as anyone ever mentioned the army he was bombarded with questions. Inevitable, really. But civilians only thought of the danger and the guns. They couldn't understand how hard it was to talk about what he'd seen. What he'd done. What he needed to leave behind. If only it was that easy. His past had a nasty habit of creeping up on him, in the middle of the night usually, snatching away sleep and leaving him ice cold.

Dan glanced over and Adam waited for the inevitable. He didn't have to wait long. 'You seen any real action?'

'Sure. Plenty.'

'Where did you go?'

'I was deployed in the hotspots—Iraq, Afghanistan, the places you've heard about but you won't be getting a postcard from any time soon. Then I was in Timor-Leste just before…' He paused. Closed down the memories. 'Before I left.'

Dan shot him a look that said *I won't ask.*

Adam was grateful for the reprieve, although he did think briefly about explaining. But, hell, he'd decided that the sooner he stopped thinking about what had happened, the sooner he'd be able to move on in his life.

The ambulance sped down the highway past the Atanga Bay turn-off. He craned his neck to look for the bright yellow medical centre. And some hint of Skye. Then realised he was being stupid.

What did he need with Little Miss Happy with a passport burning a hole in her pocket? Getting involved with her would be a quick path to disaster.

But he couldn't deny an attraction had been there. Something had stirred in him that he'd thought was forever dormant. Thought he'd seen it in her eyes too.

So it was definitely not something to pursue.

He didn't believe in some saccharin, happy-ever-after fairy-tale dream. Not after the failure of his marriage.

Not when the scars of his fallen brothers criss-crossed his heart.

Stop. His hands fisted against his seat as he reaffirmed his resolve to look forward. Looking back never achieved anything but emotional whiplash.

He focused instead on the grand colonial buildings flanking the road, the flower-festooned gardens and the acres of fields stretching out east and west from the main road. A far cry from war-torn cities with bullet-pocked buildings and the smell of death.

He sucked in sea-scented fresh air and watched palm trees sway in the gentle breeze. Living here would definitely be the tonic he'd been searching for. Once the local practice nurse had gone and his equilibrium was restored.

One SOB, a broken femur and a road traffic accident later, Adam found himself in front of Atanga Bay surgery. Confused, he turned to Dan. 'You got lost, mate? The station's back that way.'

His colleague shrugged. 'I just have a quick social call to make. Come in? I'll introduce you to the gang. It'll serve you well to get to know the local medical centres and it's a home from home here.'

Adam paused, his refusal hovering on his lips. The last few years on the move had taught him that life was easier if he kept his head down and himself to himself. People wanted to know too much, expected him to give too much.

But Dan waited with an eyebrow cocked. As a newbie to the service, turning him down would look strange. 'Sure.'

'Hi, Dan! Adam.'

Of course Skye was there. Standing in Reception as they walked in, a stethoscope hung from her neck. The dark navy uniform gave her the appearance of the true professional Adam knew she was. He got a whiff of perfume.

Something with vanilla. Subtle. An uplifting fragrance that matched her demeanour. Intoxicating. And way off limits.

'Coffee's in the percolator. There's freshly made flapjacks in the tartan tin. Go on. You know you want to.' She beamed up at them both and then focused on Adam. 'Hardly recognised you with your clothes on.'

He swallowed deeply. *This is work. Be friendly. Make an effort when others can't.* 'Thought I should wear something for the day job. Didn't want to give the patients apoplexy.' Heat prickled the back of his neck. He ran his fingers over the knots there as if easing out the tension would help with the knot in his gut. No chance.

Her pupils flared as she spoke, warm and welcoming. 'Dan will show you the way to our sparkly new staff kitchen. If you're ever passing by, you must pop in, we run an open house here. I'll be with you in a jiffy. Just got a quick blood pressure to check.'

'I'd forgotten you two had met the other day. Great nurse, even better cook.' Dan opened the tin of flapjacks and the air was filled with the aroma of golden syrup and butter. Home cooking. Not something Adam had had much on the road. His mouth watered.

And either Dan wasn't used to home baking either, or he was just darned hungry, judging by the two pieces he had in his hand. 'Quite a quirky character is our Skye. All hard on the exterior, and soft and gooey on the inside. A bit like these flapjacks, really. If you ask me, all that dark make-up's just an act. She just wants to give men the stand-off.'

'Oh?' Those black-rimmed eyes hadn't given him the stand-off, not when they'd stalked through his daydreams. No matter how much he'd tried to stop them.

Adam's stomach growled as he bit down into the oaty slice. A blast of sugar made his cheeks hurt. 'But why would she do that?'

'History, mate. Some bloke in Auckland broke her heart. She's sworn off men. Shame.'

Intrigued, Adam suddenly wanted to know more. Who? Why? And a dozen or so other things he found himself questioning about her. But gossip wasn't his style. And neither was traipsing through someone else's history. His brain worked to shut down his interest. All he wanted was a job he loved, a place of his own and not to get involved with anyone again. In any way. Anyhow.

'Good, you found it.' She flew into the room and greeted them with a flash of perfect white teeth. A regular ray of sunshine. Hell, if her smile got any brighter, he'd need to wear shades.

Having poured herself a coffee, she leaned against the sink next to Dan. 'So, Dan, you still okay for tonight?'

His colleague shifted uncomfortably and Adam's interest was piqued. A date?

Dan put his hand on Skye's shoulder and she turned to him. From this vantage point Adam watched her in profile. Long black eyelashes accentuated those huge eyes. The glint as the jewel in her nose caught the light. The swell of her full breasts. And always that wide-open smile that welcomed everyone in.

Adam felt a stirring in his gut of something he'd long forgotten. And this while she was talking about a date? With his new colleague? He stomped on his instinctive reactions. *Inappropriate.*

'No. That's why I'm here. I can't make it.' Dan looked sheepish. 'I'm really sorry, Skye. I didn't mean to let you down.'

'But you promised, Dan. We're down to two now. Just me and Connor. Mim can't do it because she's way too big. She gets uncomfortable if she can't move around.' She shook her head and Adam glimpsed a frown. 'So, there'll only be two of us. That's not going to work, is it? We need at least three or we might as well give up. The medical team needs you. It's all falling apart.'

Judging by the seriousness of their tone it was imperative that someone step up. Clearly someone with medical skills. Never one to back down from the call of duty, Adam coughed. 'Is there anything I can do to help?'

'Genius! Of course. You could do it. We need to train someone up for when I've gone anyway.' Putting her hand on his arm, she sat down on the couch next to him. She winked at Dan then turned back. She laughed and leaned in. From this angle Adam caught a glimpse of pale skin and red lace. Interesting. So not everything about her was encased in monochrome, and when she did colour it was seriously appealing.

'I only hope you're up to the job, though, Adam. It's a tough call. High pressure. Are you man enough?'

'He knows about guns and all that stuff,' Dan interjected. 'He's good on the van, knows his medicine. But I can't vouch for his knowledge and skills in other areas. You know—'

'What the hell am I getting myself into?' Adam dragged his eyes away from the distraction. Sat up straight.

His heart thudded as he glanced between the two of them. The seriousness had dissipated and he had the distinct impression he was being taken for a ride. 'Are you two winding me up? Is this some kind of initiation process, like in my new recruit days?'

'Oh? Tell all.' Her eyes widened.

'You don't want to know.'

'Another time maybe?' She sipped her coffee and held his gaze for a second. Another. Then another. A flimsy invisible thread held them locked together. He knew he shouldn't stare at her. But he couldn't help it. Something about her bright sunny smile called to a dark corner of his soul. Soothed it. Healed it slightly. Which was a stupid notion, he knew. How could a smile heal?

Then she shook her head. 'It's not a wind-up. Far from it. It's a matter of honour. And I guess you'd be good at that, being a soldier.' Did he imagine it? Did her eyes linger for a moment on his scar?

'I doubt it.' He shrugged. Ran a hand across his cheek and tried to cover the slice in his face, the permanent reminder of all he'd lost. Monica hadn't been able to look at his scar. She'd winced and turned her face away too many times. He'd believed it had reminded her of the man that had left and the shell she'd got in return.

But Skye just seemed interested in it.

Her eyes flitted away from his face and she clasped her hands in her lap. 'We're defending our eight-week championship run. Pub quiz. We're the Mad Medics.'

'The Mad…?' He shook his head. He'd been had. More people, faces, noise. More trying hard to fit in. More dodging intimacy like bullets. But he'd stepped right into the trap and couldn't back out now.

'Tonight. Eight o'clock.' She stood and beamed again. 'You just got yourself on the team.'

'You're looking very glam for a pub quiz. Hoping to dazzle the opposition into surrender? Or is it…something else? For someone else?' Connor placed a pinot gris in front of Skye and sat next to her at the small round table they'd reserved. For three. Only the third member hadn't arrived yet. Was Adam going to turn up? He'd looked dubious earlier when she'd sprung it on him.

'Oh, this old thing? It's nothing special.' She fiddled with the lace on her black top. One of the few items she'd bought on her last trip to Auckland. For ever ago.

Something for a special night out. Not that they ever happened in Atanga Bay. In the dim light of her bedroom it had looked okay. It went well with her black skinny jeans. 'Too fancy? Over the top?'

'No. It's fine. Crikey, haven't seen you so wound up for ages.'

'I'm not wound up. I just thought I'd make an effort for the team. No harm in that.' Plus the waxing, plucking to within an inch of her life, shaving, exfoliating, mud wrap. All for a darned pub quiz. She'd clearly lost her mind. She pressed a hand to her cheek, hating being the focus of attention. She'd endured too much condemnation of her appearance in the past. 'And don't be ridiculous. Since when did I dress up for anyone? I gave that useless malarkey up years ago.'

After Brian, her ex, had told her over and over that no man would ever find her attractive, so why should she bother?

Not worthy of commitment. And the insecure fool that she'd been had believed him. Put up with years of abuse because she hadn't believed she deserved better. But with a mother who cowered at the hands of her husband and a lifetime of putting her own needs after everyone else's, it had taken Skye a long time to reclaim her self-esteem and identity.

So, why the heck had she got herself decked up in lace?

She didn't want to answer that, but she hadn't imagined the way Adam had looked at her at the beach. The warmth in his eyes, even if for a second. The same warmth mirrored in her eyes. There had been a connection there, she was sure. Or was that some kind of ill-judged wishful thinking? And all of that had fed her choice of clothing—subconscious or not.

She ran her palms over her arms and bit her top lip,

trying to scrape off as much lipstick as she could. He wouldn't notice. And it didn't matter anyway, a relationship so close to her leaving would be far too complicated. And she wasn't doing that again. Complicated came with a hefty dose of hurt.

'I just thought, seeing as you've been talking non-stop about the newest member of the ambulance service…how he powered through the waves like a superhero.' Connor fluttered his eyelashes and pretended to swoon. 'How he saved poor Lukas from drowning. How he's been in the army…'

'Shut it. Last warning or time out.' She smiled through gritted teeth. Was she that transparent? Her eyes flitted to the door. Again. 'Besides, he didn't look like he wanted to come. I should have asked Sean or Stevie to fill in instead.'

'No disrespect, but your baby brothers have a combined IQ in single figures. From what I hear about Adam, he's a little more cerebral than that.'

'I wouldn't know.'

Way more, actually. And brooding. And strangely compelling to look at. With a voice that carried echoes of sadness. And softness. And strength.

She took a large slug of her wine to refocus before she got completely carried away. He was just a guy.

She knew more about them than most, having three brothers—who were simultaneously infuriating and adorable.

And her ratbag of a stepfather, and Brian, the married sleazebag. Between the two of them, they had taught her that love was made up of hurt, lies and empty promises. And not for her.

Especially not now she had three weeks and one day until that plane lifted off.

'Hi. Sorry I'm late.' The just-a-guy appeared in front of

them, dressed casually in a black T-shirt and faded jeans. He slung his leather jacket onto the back of the chair and nodded at her, his lips a straight line, his eyes guarded. He looked like he wanted to be anywhere else in the world other than a small country pub filled with laughter and friendly faces.

Edgy and dangerous and about as far away from any man she'd ever been with, or had wanted to be with before, but everything about him resonated deep inside her.

She swallowed the dry lump in her throat. 'Adam. Hi. Thought you might have had second thoughts.'

'Got a code two just before I clocked off.' Adam shrugged and glanced at Connor warily. 'That's a...'

'Serious threat to life,' Skye translated. 'This is Connor. He's one of the GPs at the surgery. The non-pregnant one, clearly. Connor, this is Adam. New paramedic about town.'

'Good to meet you.' Adam shook hands, then took his wallet out.

Connor scraped his chair back and stood. 'No. My round. By way of thanks for filling in at the last minute. You stay here and save the seats. And watch my phone— Mim's going to call if she needs me.'

'She's due any day now,' Skye explained. 'Sorry...what were you saying?'

'That it was an unlucky break, getting a last-minute callout.' Adam took the seat across from her, leaving an acre of space between them. He straightened the beermat in line with the edge of the table. Looked everywhere apart from at her face. 'I guessed everyone would know what a code two was. Being Mad Medics.'

'Sorry, did I butt in? It's a bad habit.' Her cheeks burned. She mentally banged her head against the table. 'My brothers complain because I have a tendency to—'

'Finish their sentences?' His chin jutted upwards. No

other muscles moved. Army training, she guessed. A man in control. He had a stillness that unnerved her, where she danced around and fidgeted. Adam was the kind of man who dominated a room, the one you didn't want to take your eyes off. Not that she could if she tried.

'Annoying habit, I know.'

'You'd better tell me how this quiz works. What's the strategic plan?' He scanned the groups dotted around the lounge. The aroma of male with a hint of something exotic—cinnamon perhaps—hit her as he leaned close. 'And who's the enemy?'

'Right, er, Sergeant? Corporal? I hope you don't expect military precision because you're going to be sorely disappointed.' She showed him the quiz sheets in front of her. 'Eight rounds, ten questions each round. Music, geography, current affairs, you know the score. It's more a case of luck than judgement. Or skill. Or even knowledge really.'

'I'll fit in, then.' His eyebrows rose, creasing the scar down his cheek into tiny broken lines. From here it looked well healed. Obviously old. But it would have been deep, painful. She wanted to reach out and trace it. Stupid idea.

She wanted to ask him about it too, but realised she didn't know him enough to pry about his injuries. 'So were you a captain, or a private, or what?'

'Staff sergeant medic.' His shoulders squared and his jaw twitched a little. The pale trace of light in his eyes diminished. The shutters came down.

She sensed something tragic had happened to him. She understood, knew how bruised the heart and soul could get. Maybe his abruptness wasn't lack of social grace, maybe it stemmed from something deeper.

There she was with the amateur psychology again. Still, when faced with pain and lies, she'd read as many self-help books as she could get through.

'I'm sorry if I seem nosy. Rearing three teenagers consisted of too many questions and never enough answers.' She flashed him a smile and hoped she could drag him out of whatever sombre place she'd put him with her stupid line of questioning. 'You know what boys are like, I imagine. There's enough of them in the army, eh?'

'Yeah.' His shoulders tensed. He glanced over to the bar and seemed to relax at the sight of Connor returning with the beer. Either he had a mighty thirst or he wasn't comfortable chatting with her alone.

She ran her finger round the rim of her glass and gave him her best smile. Trying to work out exactly what she felt for this just-a-guy. She came up with *confused*. He'd been relaxed with Dan, chatty with Lukas…but with her he gave little away. Other than that brief connection at the beach, he was a stranger to her.

She didn't want to get closer to him. But she sure as heck wanted to make him smile. His eyes spoke of too much pain.

Story of her life, really. Finding waifs and strays. Trying to make people smile. Putting their needs before hers. Giving up her dreams.

She dragged her eyes away from him and prayed the quiz would start soon to distract her from her wayward emotions, her wired libido and the strange effect of Adam Miller on her sensibilities.

CHAPTER THREE

THE quizmaster tapped the microphone for quiet. 'Final round. It's neck and neck. Who's going to win tonight's grand prize? Bright Sparks or Mad Medics?'

'Mad Medics, obviously.' Adam looked at the other two members of the team, chests puffed with pride, and wondered how the heck he'd got to be here, doing this. Normal things, with good people. For once the ghosts of his past hadn't spoiled his humour. 'We've got this sewn up.'

'Is that confidence or just plain cocky?' Skye leant towards him. He knew she couldn't help it as the pub had become progressively crowded as the night had worn on. There was barely enough room to move, certainly no space to avoid physical contact.

He scraped his chair back from her, didn't want to savour the enticing sensations running up and down his skin every time their arms brushed. The heat sizzling between them. He had no business enjoying being with her. Not the way his body was enjoying it anyway. 'The key is do not entertain the thought of defeat. We will win.'

'Yes, sir. I love all that who-dares-wins stuff. That's SAS isn't it? Green berets or something?' Her huge eyes stared up at him. Such innocence and interest. For the first time in four years he almost wanted to talk about his old life. Guessed she wouldn't judge. But words failed him. What if he was wrong?

He slugged back some beer. Better not to open up about anything. Keeping quiet had served him well over the years. *It had.* It might have lost him Monica, but at least his sanity was intact.

'So, ladies and gentlemen, what are you scared of? Spiders? Snakes? The number thirteen?' The quizmaster regarded each table in turn. 'Scared of losing perhaps, Mad Medics? Or just losing face? Our last round is all about phobias.'

A loud beeping was met with a wall of silence that lasted two seconds. Then shouts of *'Cheats!'*

'They're using a phone!'

'Put it away!'

Connor snatched his smartphone. His voice cracked as blood drained from his face. 'It's Mim. She's having regular contractions. Mim's having the baby. Shoot.'

He stood as cheers erupted across the room. All eyes were on the father-to-be.

'Oh, my goodness.' Skye clambered to her feet too, pale-faced, her body on alert. Primed for action. She clutched the edge of the table. 'I'll come with you.'

'Oh, no. You know what first births are like, it'll be ages yet.' Connor's mouth turned down and he raked a hand over his hair. Adam recognised the jittery voice, the shaking hands of a man half-frightened to death. 'Okay. Okay. Right. We'll be fine. You just stay here and win the quiz for us. I'll call you.'

She slicked a kiss on his cheek. 'Make sure you do. I want to be first to hear. Give her my love.'

'Okay.' Connor nodded, his eyes on Skye but his brain obviously elsewhere. Adam felt a twinge of sympathy for the man. He had a big night ahead. 'We'll be fine.'

'Now we know what he's scared of.' Adam watched as Connor pushed his way through the crowd, greeting each pat on the back with a handshake. 'The whole town seems excited about this birth. Is it something special?'

'Every birth's special.' Skye smiled. 'But Mim and Connor's baby kind of belongs to all of us. Those two are the life blood of the place.'

'As it should be.' All his life he'd been looking for this kind of community, acceptance, sharing good times. Now he'd found it he didn't know if he *could* fit in.

He'd joined up to belong to something and it had worked, for a good part of his time there. Leaving had been the right thing to do, but it had rendered him homeless in too many ways. But the community focus of Atanga Bay had a real comforting feel about it. Maybe he'd chosen the right place to settle. If he could settle at all. 'For a doctor he looks terrified.'

'For an about-to-be father I think that's probably right. How exciting.' Skye sat down, her eyes glowing. Colour rushed back into her cheeks. She had a pretty mouth, Adam noticed for the hundredth time, full lips hidden underneath a swathe of lipstick. Red. Not as dark as the other day. But glossy. Kissable.

No. She's leaving. On a jet plane.

Skye had plans. They didn't involve him. Couldn't. And he'd sworn off any kind of long-distance relationship. What chance would he have with a woman he hardly knew if his five-year marriage hadn't survived the fallout of his injury?

He didn't want to find out. Not with Skye. Even if everything about her called to him on a deep level. Had lit something inside him that he struggled to extinguish every time he spent five minutes in her company. And that appeared to be threatening to set blaze to his rationality.

She gave the pretence of biting her fingernails. 'What

a night! A labour and the quiz. No pressure, huh? Calm under fire, right? Let's bring this victory home, soldier boy.'

'Sure. No pressure. I'd rather be here than watching a woman in labour. I'm not brave enough for that.'

But now it was just a team of two. He was duty bound to stay even though every part of him strained to leave. But he couldn't leave her in the lurch and let them lose this silly pub quiz. Her black-gelled spikes tickled his head as she pored over the list of top ten most common phobias, in Latin. The lace on her top framed her pale collarbones, revealing a sweet dip he imagined running his finger along.

No. First she'd intrigued him but now it was torment just being next to the woman.

He inwardly counted to ten, scraped his chair back a fraction. Putting all thoughts of attraction to the back of his mind. Right there, out of harm's way. At the back.

She just continued her chatter, unaware of the weird sensations running through his body. Damn. Would his body stop now? Please?

He forced himself to relax, to allow the luxury of softened muscles, deeper breaths. 'Okay. Focus. What do you know about phobias?'

'Not a whole lot to be honest. Some of the names are dead giveaways. But some...I couldn't even guess.'

She pushed the list towards him. 'Look, the first three are easy. Spiders, snakes and heights. But pteromerhanophobia? Like pterodactyl? Fear of dinosaurs perhaps? Or would that be Flintstone-o-phobia? How can you be afraid of something that's extinct?'

'It's a fear of flying.' Knowing it didn't make it any easier to deal with.

Her eyes widened. 'Really? Are you sure?'

'Yes. Absolutely sure. Pteromerhanophobia, or aviatophobia.' It didn't matter which fancy name they attached to it, it all boiled down to the same thing. Terror. Falling through nothing. The screech of metal. Death.

Adam's mouth dried as adrenalin rushed through his veins. Hell, did his body have some kind of grudge against him? First his unbidden reactions to Skye, now this.

Damn. He'd got over this. The shrink had diagnosed it as PTSD, had said he'd work through it and that time healed. He was running out of patience.

Pull yourself together, Miller.

He focused on the pain in his ankle, controlled his breathing, flexed his foot on the floor. Hard surface. The pub's solid foundations beneath his feet. Reminded himself he needn't fly anywhere soon. Ever again, if he could help it.

Semper quietus. Always calm. Whoever had thought that motto up hadn't taken a skydive from a burning chopper without a parachute.

When he looked over at Skye she was blissfully ignorant of his discomfort. Her forehead creased as she pored over the questions. A study in concentration. A study in sensuality as she tapped the end of the pencil against her cheek. The black of the graphite stark against the pale cream of her flesh. Sense took over. They had a time limit on this round.

Concentrate. He hauled in a breath of beer-soaked oxygen and took hold of the pencil to stop his hand from shaking, filled in the gaps on the form. 'Yes, it's definitely a fear of flying. You're right, named after the pterodactyl I presume, the dinosaur bird thing.'

'Wow. Well done. Any others?'

He settled into a change of subject. 'Trypanophobia is a fear of needles.'

'And you know that because…?'

'We had a lot of new-recruit fainters. Wanted to learn how to kill a man with their bare hands but couldn't stomach a tiny needle in their arms.'

'I'm impressed. Go you. So, *cynophobia*…any ideas?' She pointed a slim finger at him. 'We're so close to winning this darned thing.'

'I haven't a clue. I guess everyone's scared of something. What other things are people afraid of? What about you?'

'Me? Oh…nothing.' For once her smile slipped. Her mouth puckered as she thought. From the hesitant look in her eyes he knew there was a lot more to it than that. He recognised a hedged answer when he saw it.

'Oh, come on. There must be something. The dark? Creepy-crawlies? Monsters?'

'Nothing. I can't think…'

She'd been hurt somehow—by that man in Auckland, no doubt—and she might believe she hid it well, but that sunny smile didn't fool him.

He knew how to put on a brave face like the rest of them. When everything around was crashing down. When even silence was unbearable. When you didn't think you could stand the pain any more. But you had to. Because at least you were still alive. Then when the physical pain stopped, the guilt rose like black smoke, filled the gaps.

She shrugged. 'Okay. My phobia? Clipping my wings. Staying in Atanga Bay for ever. Not seeing the rest of the world before I die. I don't want to be hemmed in. Is that claustrophobia, then? You?'

'Is there such a thing as pub-quiz-ophobia? I'm getting real close to that.' He watched the smile on her face grow and enjoyed the jolt of pride for putting it back there.

'Time's up. Now I'll do the marking.' Mike collected the paper.

'Excuse me.' Someone tapped Adam's shoulder. He stood, snapping his heels together, almost to attention. Then eased off. Some habits took too long to die. Four years later and his body still locked on command. He almost laughed. He was face to face with a surfer in a pub, not on parade. 'You're the guy from the other day, right? The beach? You pulled me out?'

Adam's heart lifted at the sight of Lukas, his arm in a sling and a bandage round his head. 'Hey, mate. You were bleeding like a stuffed pig. We saved you from being some shark's dinner. Good to see you. You okay?'

'Great.' He lifted his sling. 'Broken arm and ten stitches to the head. Can I buy you a drink to say thanks?'

'If you insist.' Within minutes three pints sat in front of him courtesy of Lukas, Lukas's father and the pub owner, Lukas's uncle. Adam stared at the drinks in dismay. 'Seems such a waste. I'll never drink all these.'

'They want to show their appreciation, it's our way.' Skye waited for the next round of handshaking to diminish before speaking. Surprised to see the cool and calm soldier ruffled under the spotlight. 'You're quite a hero, Adam. Wallow in it for a while.'

'I said before, I'm no hero. Seriously.' His voice rose slightly. She'd heard that hitch before, seen that look in her brothers' eyes more than once. For the loss of their mother. For a mate killed in a car crash. Hurt hidden deep. What surprised her was how much it affected her.

She'd only known him a handful of hours over the course of a few days, and yet his pain reverberated through her soul. Met her hurt head on. They had a shared loss, she sensed, understood each other at a deep level, even though neither had the means to admit it.

She fought an instinctive urge to put her hand on his. To wrap him in her arms and soothe the pain with touch.

But he wasn't her brother. Her lover. She had no right to touch him.

He took a long drink and seemed to will himself to relax. 'Sorry, that came out wrong. I meant I was just doing my job.'

'Well, you did it well. You know, you should focus more on the positives.'

'Is that what your perennial smiling's about?'

'I try. No point being glum.' She nodded and beamed at him just to prove her point. 'We have to make the best of things. Life's way too short. Seize the day. And any other glib clichés you can think of.'

'Is that why you're so keen to go off travelling?'

'It's a long story and I won't bore you with the details. Suffice it to say, I need a break.'

'Then take it.' The way he nodded at her, like he understood, was disconcerting.

'Everyone else has all but begged me to stay. Especially my brothers. Who will cook? Clean? Remind them to do stuff?'

'How about they do it for themselves?'

'I hear you. I've been telling them that for years. Falls on deaf ears.'

'Shout louder. Or just keep on talking. You appear to be very good at that.' His mouth twitched. 'Do whatever it takes, but go on your adventure.'

'No one else understands why I need to get away. I just want to have the same kind of fun every other twenty-something has.' She'd had her time to nurse, to grieve, to parent far too young.

She could see in his eyes that Adam knew how it felt to want to run away from responsibility. But he was tight-lipped as ever. 'For as long as I stay here I will be needed. I don't want to be needed any more.'

'You're a nurse, you'll be needed for as long as you practise.'

'Like you, I guess. First a soldier and now a paramedic. You have such a worthwhile job that will make a huge difference to people's lives.'

'Now you're making me sound like the Dalai Lama.' The corners of his mouth turned up. Just a little. Stretching muscles that looked lax from lack of use. Then, like butterfly wings unfurling after a long incubation, a slow smile spread across his lips. It looked like it was something his face wasn't used to doing. Like he'd forgotten how. Even in her darkest moments she'd made herself focus on the good things, had never forgotten how to smile.

But it turned his features from granite to something more…beautiful. Alluring. Interesting. Transformed him from unconventionally attractive to insanely sexy. 'Maybe I should become a monk.'

'No. You wouldn't suit the orange robes. So not your colour.' A celibate monk would be a terrible waste of such a sublime man.

She leaned back and watched the puzzlement on his face. The shadows lifted but a little frown line indented his forehead. He was delicious to observe. Especially when he grappled with her humour. Tingles ran the length of her spine. Amazing that a fledgling smile could do that. Make you forget everything. Make you want things out of reach. 'And you'd have to live in a cave like a hermit. In silence or something. With no facilities. Or in a monastery with lots of hymns. Very dull.'

'But imagine, no one to force pints on me. No pub quizzes. Very tempting.' Then he laughed. It was like setting something free. His face transformed into a boyish picture of unhaunted innocence. His head tipped back and a deep resonant rumble came from his chest. A soulful sound that reached down to her heart and squeezed.

'See, smiling works. Don't deny you feel better.'

'My mouth hurts.' He grimaced, then his smile softened. He ran a hand along his stubbled jaw. It was almost as if he was feeling the strangeness of his stretched features, and for some strange reason her eyes followed his fingers closely, every movement. Transfixed by the haunting beauty of his hewn face. The scar that drew her gaze and made her want answers to the many questions buzzing round her head.

Who are you? The reluctant hero, the stubbornly serious and obviously haunted man. A man who could warm her with one look of his hesitant gaze. But a man who could laugh too. It had taken time, but he had started to soften. Maybe only just a little, but there was potential there. And she sure as hell wanted to see that face light up again, and soon.

A loud bleeping made her jump. Skye grabbed for her phone. 'It's a text message. From Connor.' Fear and excitement mixed inside her stomach. 'Oh, God, they need help. He says: *"Baby's coming. Midwife delayed. Mim needs you."*

'I've got to go.' She stood, picked up her bag then had another thought. 'Do you want to come?'

'Will they want me there? What about the quiz…?' But he'd already grabbed his jacket. Despite his denial about being any kind of hero, she knew him well enough that he would never turn down a chance to help out in an emergency.

'We'll have to get the score tomorrow. How are your midwifery skills?'

'Rusty. I did some deliveries in rural Timor-Leste.' He

stiffened, his face back in shadows, then he shrugged as they worked their way through the bar. 'You?'

'Needs work,' she admitted. 'But between us we'll sort it. Two doctors, a paramedic and a nurse. If we can't do it, no one can.'

A swirl of humidity hit them as they opened the door. Adam threw his jacket over his shoulder. 'Poor Mim labouring in this heat. I hope it goes okay.'

'Don't you know anything?' She nudged him towards the car park. Resisting the temptation to lean against him. *'Do not entertain the thought of defeat.'*

'You're a fast learner.'

'Oh, believe me. I can be.'

His hand knocked against hers and their fingers curled for a second before he pulled away. She savoured the moment, a large bear paw of a hand with rough fingertips. A work-worn hand. A real man's hand. A hand that could hold a heart secure and safe. She'd seen those hands at work, knew the tender and skilled way they'd saved Lukas.

After her jog.

After her countdown had begun properly.

Her heart stilled, and as they walked to her car she sped ahead out of touching distance. Being this close to him gave her disturbing thoughts. Challenged her plans. Made her want something out of reach.

No. No point getting too deep into something she wouldn't be able to extricate herself from further down the track. Three weeks and one day didn't leave a lot of time for anything, and certainly not for something that would inevitably lead to heartache one way or another.

CHAPTER FOUR

'HEY, beautiful, in a hurry to have this baby?' Skye down-graded her frantic dash to an efficient stride as she found Mim in the lounge of their home. Connor hovered around her, looking delighted and petrified in equal measure.

At the sight of her best friend screwed up, red-faced and in obvious pain, Skye pushed all thoughts of Adam from her brain. Mim was her priority now. But she couldn't erase the image of his grinning face, so liberated and free, from her scattered mind.

She knelt near Mim's head as her friend curled into a ball and they all watched, helpless, as another contraction washed over her.

When the shaking stopped Mim held out her hand and gripped Skye's. 'Don't *beautiful* me,' she gasped, through dry lips. 'I look like a beached whale about to explode.'

'No, you don't.' Skye wiped her palm across her friend's forehead, slicked her sticky fringe out of her eyes. Knowing the complicated journey Mim and Connor had had to get this far made the promise of her baby arriving imminently all the sweeter. 'You're as lovely as ever, and going to be a mum really soon.'

'Who's this? The famous Adam?' Her friend looked over at Adam, who had been standing apart from them, at the threshold. The smile had long since left his face, but now he wore a quizzical look. No doubt wondering what he'd let himself in for. His eyes were calm yet alert.

Skye's breath hitched a little and blood rushed to her face. Just looking at him seemed to have a strange autonomic effect on her body. Which was annoying; in all her dealings with men over the years, none of them had made her blush on sight. None.

Stop that.

'Yes. I'm Adam, guilty as charged. Hi, there, Mim.' He stepped into the room, squeezed passed Connor and crouched next to Skye. His heat and smell washed over her, familiar and exciting. A hum charged round her body as if it knew instinctively what pleasures and promises lay under that dark T-shirt.

She shifted to give him room, making sure a sedate few centimetres lay between her and temptation. He nodded at her and crouched to look over their patient. However uncomfortable he may have felt about sharing one of the most intimate times in the human condition, he didn't show it. 'You're doing great. Not long to go.'

Mim waved feebly. 'Skye's told me all about you. She's right, you are gorgeous.'

Please, no. Not here. Not now. Not ever. Heat emanated from Skye's cheeks. 'No, you're not.'

Ouch. Realising how that had sounded, her blush deepened into a total body flush. 'I mean...you are, but— Ignore the pregnant lady, she's delusional. It's the hormones.'

'Sure, no worries.' Relief skittered across his granite features, leaving a trace of warmth in his eyes. She could have sworn another smile threatened, but then it disappeared. Now was not the time for him to know she had the hots for his body. And who wouldn't? It was damn near perfect. She'd be a cold fish if she hadn't noticed that. Noticing didn't mean a thing.

Mim winced again, her face contorting. 'Owwwwwww.'

Skye knew the instant Adam clicked from just friendly to paramedic mode. His jaw muscle tensed and his voice smoothed as he spoke, emanating authority and cool-headedness, 'It's okay, Mim. Breathe through it. That's right. Well done. You're doing really well.'

'I was going to drive to the hospital, but her contractions are getting too close together.' Connor held his wife's hand as the pain eased. 'I called the ambulance, but they're going to be a while. Busy night.'

'Any idea how far dilated you are?' Adam rubbed a hand over his chin as he smiled, very minutely, at Mim. For Mim it was soft and careful. For Skye it had been generous and unfettered. Either way he smiled. He'd gone from a fledgling grin to a selection of smiles in a matter of hours. Blood heated in her abdomen as she watched the gentle transformation.

'Don't know. I should check.' Connor made to move.

Mim's body tensed. 'No. Stay. Here. My back hurts. Rub...'

With a strange sense of pride Skye watched Adam step forward and put a palm on Connor's shoulder. The soon-to-be dad looked spooked and torn but relaxed a little as Adam took him to one side. 'I don't know how you all want to do this. And please tell me if I'm out of line, but your wife needs you to hold her hand. To be dad and husband at this moment, rather than doctor. Is that okay with you?'

Perfect choice of words.

'Yes. Please. I. Need. You. Here.' Mim began to pant as another contraction racked her body.

'So how about Skye and I stay down the business end? At least for now. If I'm in any way concerned I'll tell you, I promise.'

Connor nodded. 'There's a sterile pack over there. I

don't have anything else much. An emergency delivery pack would have been nice. But—'

'That's good for starters. We'll manage.'

'You think? I want drugs. An epidural. Pethidine. Gas and air. Knock me out.' Mim doubled up again, swaying her body left and right, getting lost in that trance-like place Skye had seen women go to. Deep within themselves, in a primitive response to exactly what their body was doing.

She helped Mim change position. 'You want to go upstairs? The bed might be more comfortable.'

'Can't. Walk.'

'We'll stay here, then.' After she'd checked Mim's progress she patted her friend's hand, trying to keep calm when she knew by the speed of this labour they possibly had minutes, an hour tops. 'You're fully dilated. This baby's coming, ready or not.'

'I'm. Not. Ready.' Mim panted through the pain, the timing and intensity of contractions increasing almost at fever pitch.

'Sure you are. Try to relax.'

'I can't relax. I'm having a baby and it hurts. Connor!' Mim panted the words through gritted teeth. 'Connor. You. Owe. Me. Big time.'

'Transition?' Skye glanced over to Adam, who nodded back to her. He opened his mouth to speak, but seemed to think better of it. Again. He was a man of few words, but when he spoke it meant everything.

She watched those lips work, wondering fleetingly how soft they'd be to touch. Then her eyes slid over his fascinating face and caught his gaze. The blue irises were flecked with gold and a flash of heat stoked her insides. How could someone she'd only known a few days affect her so deeply?

She held his gaze for as long as she dared, a simmering connection growing between them as fast as Mim's contractions.

Then she set about preparing for the delivery.

Show time. Adrenalin jolted Adam into action. He dragged his eyes away from Skye and refocused his attention.

Mim. Almost term. With no complications in her pregnancy. That he knew of. So he should expect a safe, simple delivery. Although precipitous labours could cause shock for the mother, they rarely caused problems for the child.

Rolling up his sleeves, he scrubbed his hands in the bathroom basin, then dashed back to the sofa. Put on more gloves. 'Baby's crowning, you don't hang around, do you?'

'No! Owwww.'

He watched Skye fuss around her friend. As well as monitoring vital signs as best she could with little equipment, she'd stretched clean towels over the floor, lit candles, found relaxing music and somehow summoned a cosseting breeze through billowing curtains. If ever there was a haven to give birth in, this was it. She was in her element, her cheeks pink with excitement, her lips half-parted in concentration as she whispered soothing words to Connor and Mim. She seemed to know exactly what they all needed. And provided it all, along with her usual happy demeanour.

She glanced over at him and winked conspiratorially. Her lips twitched upwards and he felt his own doing the same. Seemed her damned smiling was infectious all of a sudden.

He couldn't get involved here. Not any deeper than he already was, so far out of his comfort zone he was in enemy territory. The only way out was to retreat as far as he could.

So, positioning himself to help the baby's grand entrance, he put himself back in a safe place. 'Copy my breaths, Mim. Pant-pant-blow. Again. That's it. Again. Hold on. When the urge to push is so strong you can't deny it any more, then we'll do it. Okay? Not before.'

'I can't.'

'Sure you can. It's what women are designed to do. Trust your body.'

'I can't. You don't understand. I'm scared.'

He dug deep, knowing all eyes were on him. Knowing Mim needed him. Connor took her weight under her shoulders, Skye crouched, holding Mim's hands, all breaths held as they waited for Adam to take command. Mim's hands shook, her face screwed up in fear and agony.

He knew how that felt. Remembered that fear overwhelmed, stopped any rational thought. Pushed reasoning aside. Fear and pain had sent him under.

He breathed with her. Drew on his own experiences to help. Brought forth all the strength he could. 'I know all about scared, Mim. I know how that feels. Believe me, I understand. But take that fear and use it for good. You can do this.'

'I can't. It hurts.'

'Put all those feelings into positive energy.' Easier said than done. His pulse rate soared and he forced it to slow. She needed him to stay absolutely calm. 'I know you can. I know you can. You'll be meeting baby very soon.'

'I need to push.' She sucked in a breath. 'Bloody. Hell. Soorrrrry.'

'I've been sworn at in so many languages I could write a dictionary. Give it all you've got.'

'Okay…' Tranquillity surrounded Mim as she nodded, eyes closed, rocking to a rhythm only she could hear. Primed to ride the next contraction. Ready for her new baby. 'Help me. Nooooow.'

Throwing her head back and scrunching her face tight, Mim bore down, grunting.

A second. A scream. Two shoulders.

And out slithered a slick, bawling…

'Girl, it's a girl.' Skye assisted Connor to catch the baby. 'Your baby is a girl. She's beautiful and has a fine pair of lungs.'

Counting the fingers and toes, quickly checking her over for any obvious concerns, Adam helped them lift the jerking bundle onto her mother's stomach. Wondering then what he could use to clamp and cut the cord, he stepped away from the couch and scanned the room.

'You looking for this?' Beside him Skye held out a clamp, knowing what he needed.

After he'd watched as Connor proudly cut the cord, Adam turned back to Skye. Tears glistened in her eyes and her bottom lip wobbled. A primal need to look after her sprang out of nowhere.

His hand found its way to her damp cheek. She tilted her chin to look up into his eyes and, for a second, the temptation to smooth his mouth over hers almost ate him away. But he fought it. Needed to keep things level. Couldn't risk where anything more might lead. But he couldn't stand by and watch her cry. 'Hey, you okay?'

'I'm just being silly. Emotional, you know. It's always special, eh?' She rocked her cheek in his palm and her eyes fluttered closed for a second. A picture of peace.

Damn. He'd mastered stand-offish. Isolated the shrapnel pieces left of his heart. But something about Skye made him want to stay like this. At peace with a beautiful woman. In this cocoon of bonding and babies and everything out of reach.

No point in getting soft. He shouldn't let himself get carried away. He let his hand drop.

'Oh.' Her eyes fluttered open and he saw the questions there, the hurt at his abruptness, and was ashamed he'd put that uncertainty in her mind.

He turned away from her and all that fresh emotion brimming in her face. Emotional? And then some. Together they'd shared something special, witnessed a miracle, a new life. And because of that the connection between them had cemented into something more tangible. A real force.

Without bidding, his thoughts turned to those who would never see a child born, or hold loved ones in their arms, and the chances he'd lost to have this for himself.

A rock, as big as Mount Noshaq, lodged in his throat, reminding him of how foolish it was to get involved. With a woman. With Skye.

Not unless he wanted to fall right off the deep end.

He hadn't spent the last four years shunning contact, skittering from town to town, building bricks around his heart just to have her knock them down again.

'Thanks for the drive home. And for everything you did for Mim and Connor.' Skye opened Adam's truck door but hesitated to climb out immediately. Some weird unfinished business hung around them. Something had deepened. Closer yet not closer. Perhaps she'd imagined it.

'Hey, no worries. It was my pleasure. I'm always happy with a safe delivery.' His eyebrows rose, making his eyes widen, the deep, deep blue drawing her in. 'Not sure I can cope with so much excitement in one day, though. I'll watch you to your door.'

As she climbed out of the car a cool breeze washed over her, allowing her to breathe deeply. Being in close quarters with Adam had had her flailing for oxygen. After the way he'd dropped his hand from her cheek and shut down she realised he was struggling with this as much as she was.

She didn't need uncertainty. History repeating itself. *Does he, doesn't he? Will he, won't he?* Brian had enjoyed his silly games that had made him powerful and her powerless. What had begun as a delicious adventure had worn her down to a mess with the self-esteem of a gnat. It had taken her years to claw back confidence and she sure as heck didn't want to get lost again before she embarked on her trip.

A bright yellow moon lit up the midnight sky and illuminated the path to her front door. She should take it, one quick step after another. She didn't.

Adam wasn't Brian. He was a colleague and he'd done a lot for her friends. Maybe she should let go of her insecurities and remember her manners. She leaned back into the car.

'Would you like to come in for a nightcap? I have some Scotch somewhere. Don't know about you, but I'm still wired. I'll never get to sleep.'

'I don't think so. Not tonight.' He gave her the kind of smile he'd given Mim earlier. She'd been downgraded. To gentle. 'Another time maybe?'

'Okay, silly idea. I should just go straight to bed. Count sheep, or newborn babies or something.'

'Er…' He glanced at his watch, his face a picture of indecision grappling with common sense. 'Okay. Just one. After the beer earlier I'd better watch it.'

If her brothers thought it strange she'd brought a man home at way past bedtime they didn't show it. But they all slunk off to bed.

Her heart sank at the beer cans littering the kitchen table, the almost empty yoghurt cartons oozing onto the mats, stray socks in odd places. Oily rags cluttered the sideboard and a stack of old motorbike magazines had obviously crashed to the floor and no one had bothered to pick them up. Her house looked like she felt, a crazy jumble of chaos. 'Just look at the place! I'm so sorry about the mess. We're still at the house-training stage. It's taking longer than I thought.'

'And they're how old?'

'Eighteen, nineteen and twenty. I hope Mim does better with her little one.' She sighed and collected the empty cartons into her arms, silently cursing her irresponsible brothers. 'There's an eight-year gap between me and Sean, the oldest one. Then Mum was apparently in a hurry to get the family completed.'

Adam frowned as his eyes shot from the pile in her arms to the table and back. 'What exactly are you doing?'

'Clearing up.'

The frown deepened into a scowl. 'Why?'

'Because it's a mess.'

'Put them down.'

'Sorry?'

His index finger commanded exactly where she should put them. 'Put them down right now, and step away from the mess.'

'Yes, sir.' In shock she dumped them all back onto the table. 'They should have made you a major general with a pointy finger like that.'

'You need more than a pointy finger to be a major.' Those lovely lips twitched.

'Oh, yeah? Like what? Clicky heels and a penchant for medals?' Her heart squeezed as he pressed his knuckles against his mouth. *Just let go.* 'Watch it, Adam. I think there's a smile threatening. What should we do? Duck and cover?'

'Come on, it's not that unusual for me to smile.'

'No? I've never known a man find it so hard to kick back.'

'I kick back.' He sat down at the table, opposite her. He didn't seem affronted by her comments, just intrigued. She sensed he'd lost something a long time ago and was struggling to find it. 'Sometimes.'

'Try make a habit out of it. You never know, you might get to like it. Life doesn't have to be serious all the time.' Or maybe she was wrong. Maybe it was his nature to be serious, maybe she should back right off, concentrate on the promise of delicious French men and scintillating Italians, instead of battle-scarred Kiwis who didn't want to smile.

He peered at her from the corner of his eye, guarded, yet warm. 'Who are you, my mother?'

'No, just a girl who hates dwelling on the bad stuff.'

'And your answer for that is what? Keep smiling and hope everything gets better?'

She placed her hands on the table, palms down. 'Think of your life as a novel. If you don't like what's happening, write yourself a different chapter.'

'It's an idea.' An eyebrow peaked.

'A damned good one.'

'That easy?'

'That easy.' At least, that's what she'd been telling herself for years.

He nodded and a smile grew, flickering across his scar and all the way up to his eyes.

Until he glanced at the detritus on the table. He picked up a sock between two pinched fingers and sighed. 'Not *my* mother, but theirs. Really? They can't take their own dirty laundry out? It's late, you've been working all day. No doubt you fixed dinner for them too, right?'

'Right.'

'Then you delivered a baby. You have dark circles under your eyes, you're trying desperately hard to do everything for everyone. You're tired and wound up.'

How could he see what no one else saw? What she felt? Her shoulders sagged. 'Yes. I'm bushed. But that doesn't stop the fact that things need to be done.'

'Do you have pen and paper?'

She grabbed some from a drawer in the kitchen console. 'Why?'

'Leave this on the table.' He scribbled something in precise neat handwriting and handed it to her.

Maid service no longer applies. Get your acts together, or get another place to live.

'And give it three days. After that, anything still lying around gets thrown away.'

'No!' She looked at him in horror, although a bubble of laughter erupted from her throat. 'I can't...can I?'

'Of course you can. This is your house too. I guess you do most of the work. The least they can do is help out.'

Could she? Put her foot down and bring an end to their slovenliness? Hell, yes. She could. 'They'll hate me. Can I put *"Sorry"* on the end?'

'Absolutely not. Why are you sorry that you're going to facilitate them to become fully functioning members of the human race? You make a mess, you clear it up. It's not rocket science.' Sitting the note in the middle of the table, he sat back and studied her reaction. 'They're old enough to know better. They'll respect you.'

Respect—now, there was a word foreign to her vocabulary. 'Some chance. It's been hard for them. Dad—their dad, my stepdad...' She shuddered. He'd been nothing like a father to her. A brute and a bully. Big, like Adam, but with none of Adam's quiet grace or calm. 'Walked out a few years ago, when Mum got diagnosed with ovarian cancer. He said he couldn't take the pressure.'

'Classy.'

'Then she died. The boys were devastated. We all were.' All the jumbled emotions of today and of those last few days with her mother meshed into a tight knot in her chest. It was too late at night to be speaking about such things, but somehow Adam's composed face and soft voice made her want to talk. She kept the sadness at bay, down in that deep, safe place she never opened. 'I came back to nurse her, to be here for them all.'

'You gave up your job? That was a huge sacrifice. Have any of them ever thanked you for it?' There he was, teasing facts out of her she hadn't wanted to share with anyone else. Usually she had no problem skimming over the details of her life. She just kept the pain hidden behind a perpetual smile. That way it didn't hurt.

'I'm all they have and I wanted to do things for them, to make them feel better. It's been hard for us all.' She dragged in a deep breath and stood. 'Now, where's that whisky?'

She lifted two crystal glasses and a bottle from the cabinet, and glugged a decent shot of thick amber liquid into each. A smile fixed on lips that felt taut. 'Of course, I wouldn't have missed those last years with Mum for anything.'

When she sat again she realised Adam's chair had somehow twisted and he was opposite her, close, knees touching hers. His proximity confused her heightened senses.

His strong hands cupped the glass, his head tilted to one side. The concern on his face took her breath away. She met his eyes and that connection fired between them. He understood her pain, but it was more than that. His look offered her comfort. And more. Much more. Things she didn't want to think about, didn't want to put a name to.

He swirled the whisky round in his glass, took a sip. 'Looking after her must have been hard.'

'It was an honour.' She grappled for a breath, trying to swallow round the brick in her throat. Her thoughts scrambled between the sadness of her mother and a sudden dangerous need for Adam. She dragged her eyes away from him and tried to focus on the future. The uncomplicated future she'd planned. The one that didn't involve grumpy paramedics.

'My mum fuelled my dreams. She always wanted to travel. She gave me scrapbooks she'd made over the years, postcards from people and pictures of places we found in our world atlas.' She pulled one of her scrapbooks from the shelf and opened at her favourite page. Took refuge in its familiarity and the promise of her trip there soon. She smoothed down the well-thumbed ratty corners. 'The Duomo in Florence. The Ponte Vecchio. Michelangelo's *David*. All that yummy pasta. Gelato to die for.'

'Yeah, it's pretty awesome. Try the *espresso* flavour. The best.'

'You've been?'

'To Italy, yes, and a whole lot of other places too. You get to see the world in my job.' He paused. 'My old job.'

'And you don't want to go back? To Europe, at least?' A tentative plan began to hatch. A half-idea that wasn't properly formed, ethereal, like a ghost, just out of reach. Wishful thinking and a whole lot of jumbled thoughts.

His face shadowed and all at once that plan fizzled into nothing. 'No. I've done all of that. I've spent nigh on fifteen years moving from one place to the next. One country to the next. I need to put my roots down somewhere.'

'I'm tired of roots. I want adventure.' It had been all she'd ever wanted. Everything she'd worked for over the last few years. Halted by Brian's demands. Her mother's

illness. Her brothers' needs. Bad timing all round. That
and bad judgement, taking a punt on the wrong kind of
guy. Truth was, she didn't think there was a right kind.
She shut the scrapbook. 'The boys don't want me to go.'

'I'm not surprised. I wouldn't want you to go either.'

'Oh?' Her heart jerked a little, wondering what he meant
by such a bold statement. Was it her imagination or had he
leant a fraction closer? His fresh male scent reached her
senses. So different from the tangy smell of boys, Brian's
cloying cologne, her stepdad's sweat. Adam had an earthy
scent, fresh air, the sea. Sex.

She inhaled and allowed her imagination to wander
along a dangerous path, with deep crevasses on either side.
She didn't want to think like this, imagine he might be attracted to her. Imagine what it might be like to have him
hold her. And more. It hadn't worked out too well last
time she'd been down that route and she'd ended up with
nothing but pain.

'They won't be able to cope without you. You do way
too much for them. How about you write a new chapter
for everyone in this house?'

'I have.' She let the breath out slowly. Re-routed to a
safer course. 'It's entitled, *"I'm leaving"*.'

'Yes, you are.' He pushed the scrapbook behind him, out
of sight. His hands reached to her face, stretching work-
worn fingers along her hairline and very gently pulling her
towards him. When her face was a heartbeat away from
his he whispered into her ear. His breath sent shivers along
her spine, pooling in her abdomen where a fire raged. 'So
this is going to be a very dumb move.'

CHAPTER FIVE

VANILLA filled the air around him. Drunk on the smell and fuelled by the whisky, Adam inched closer. 'But, God knows, I can't help it.'

Skye's dark eyes stayed locked on his, an expression of surprise and desire written there. She didn't pull away. She didn't move an inch.

He wanted her. The urge to wrap his hands around her curves almost threatened to suffocate him. The thought blew him away. He hadn't been prepared for this.

A drink, sure. A friendly nightcap between colleagues. But not this. This insatiable need for her, risen out of nowhere. Out of her smile, and her voice and hidden sadness that he could see even though she tried to bury it. Out of the misguided love she showed her brothers and the unquestioning loyalty to her family. The need to be loved and cared for. It should have set alarm bells ringing. But he wanted a piece of her optimistic spirit. Of her.

He scraped his chair forward and slid his knees to either side of her thighs, fitted himself into her space. His heart raged a thunderous beat as he took what he'd been aching for since the moment he'd seen her.

He pressed his lips onto her mouth. Dumb?

And then some. But since when had he ever played safe?

A moment's hesitation and a quiet 'Oh' then her arms

snaked up and round his neck. Her soft body pressed against him, firing lust-shaped arrows to his groin. Four years and of all the women he'd been with no one had come close to igniting so much as a flicker. And then along came Skye.

The moment his lips touched hers doubt and confusion disappeared. Thought and reasoning melted away. Her mouth shaped to his. Her lips were soft and yielding, chaste almost. He traced tiny kisses along her mouth, wanting to be gentle, to lead her along a path filled with tenderness.

Slowly. Slowly, for both their sakes. Although the ache in his groin and the acid in his veins warned him of his intense need. A need that had germinated when he'd first seen her and had swelled ever since.

She slid forward tentatively, straddled his thighs and opened her mouth to him, more confident now as a quiet moan escaped her throat. Her innocent playfulness cemented to something more intense, passionate. 'Adam. You taste so good.'

'God.' His hands moulded to her back as he pressed against her, feeling the sensual dips and curves of her spine, the slope of her bottom, the rasp of black lace against his skin.

A tiny uncertain flick of her tongue against his reminded him of how unsure she'd seemed. How much hurt she'd endured at the hands of her father and her ex.

A kiss didn't promise a lifetime, but to Adam it meant a commitment of sorts. Not *wham, bam, thank you, ma'am.* Not for Skye.

She deserved better. She deserved someone who was capable of sharing her life. Someone different. He couldn't travel with her and he wouldn't think about her staying.

He couldn't do a short fling, however tempting, not with someone who evoked such intense emotions in him.

He pulled back, cupped her cheek. 'We can't… I'm sorry.'

Her smile slipped as she stared at the space he'd made then bit the corner of her bottom lip. Once again hesitation and confusion flashed across her eyes. Her breathing levelled. She slid back and stood up. 'Sorry for what?'

'For taking advantage. Kissing you. I shouldn't have. It's not right.'

'Seemed fine to me. Better than fine.' But she didn't look fine as she turned away. The moment was gone. A bucket of virtual cold water splashed over his lust. Made icy by the flat smile he knew she'd fixed on her face just to make him feel better. 'Is this some kind of game to you?'

'What? You think I'm messing with you?' Stringing her along? *Dumb move all round, Miller.* 'No. I don't play games. I should have stopped.'

'You did stop.' She gathered up the cans and empty pots from the table and threw them in the bin, swatted the socks towards the laundry door, thumbing her defiance to his previous playful order. Her back was rigid and her voice polite. 'Whatever else you may think of me, please understand that I don't usually kiss people I hardly know in my kitchen. You should go. Thanks for the ride home.'

'Okay. But—'

'And a kiss is just a kiss, so they say. Forget it.'

Unlikely. He shrugged on his jacket, a zillion phrases running through his head. Useless platitudes, all of them. 'Skye, kissing leads to other things. Things that would be confusing for us both. I can't do anything serious and definitely not long distance. It's doomed before we begin.'

'I don't remember asking for serious. No big deal. And there is no *it*.' She ushered him out of the kitchen and opened the front door, her eyes burning. Behind her bravado he saw hurt, questions and damaged pride. 'Please, don't mention this to anyone.'

'Of course not. I'm sorry.'

'We're both adults. Got a little carried away, I guess. Too much emotion for one night. Should have just gone straight to bed when I got home.' This time her weak smile seemed genuine. 'That came out wrong.'

He tried to make light of it, to squeeze off the weight in his chest. 'Thought it might be an invite?'

'No. I don't do one-night stands. I've got more self-respect than that. And getting involved with someone when I've three weeks before I leave would be insane.' Her chin tilted, an action he guessed she'd worked at as it didn't come naturally. The slight tremor in her hands and the crack in her voice hadn't gone unnoticed. It almost broke his resolve, seeing her trying to be so nonchalant. And failing.

'Don't worry, Adam, I'm not the clingy sort.'

And this was her kiss-off. He should be relieved. How many times had he dredged up some poor excuse to save face and escape commitment? *It's not you, it's me.*

This time was different, she was saying it and letting him go. No questions asked. He hovered on the threshold, unable to leave without some gesture of reconciliation. 'Maybe we could hang out together for a drink some time.'

'To what end?'

'To get to know you better. To stop things being awkward.'

Right now anything would feel better than the acre of space between them. He'd hurt her and he hadn't meant to. Just charged in without thinking what it would mean. The first time he hadn't thought things through, assessed the danger. The first time, and it had ended in trouble. That'd teach him.

But he wanted to put that megawatt smile back on her face. And he got the feeling he could only do that by treating her well, making her understand how special she was.

She chewed on the inside of her cheek. 'Why would you want to get to know me better when we're on a hiding to nothing here?'

'I thought it'd be nice. It's not like you to be mistrusting.'

'Only with strange men on my doorstep after midnight.' She held her palm up to him. 'I'm sorry, it's been a hell of a day and I'm tired.'

He glanced up at a light in the bedroom above. Guessed one of her brothers was keeping watch. He lowered his voice. 'I like you, Skye with an "e". You're a good person.'

'Sure I am.' She nodded then began to close the door, her voice a muffled whisper but her words rang loud and clear in his head as he walked away. 'I'm just not someone you want to kiss.'

The moment Skye replaced the phone on the handset she knew she'd invited trouble. Two days and she'd seen nothing at all of Adam. But instinct told her it would be he who would answer her emergency transfer call.

After their kiss she'd spent a sleepless night trying to erase the excitement and heat he'd generated in her, and the disappointment at him ending it. But she'd resurrected what little pride she had managed to salvage after her ex had squashed it into his mangy tutor-room carpet, and vowed not to let her wayward lust get the better of her. Easy to do when the man you want to kiss didn't want to kiss you back.

Why had he kissed her? Why the heck had she kissed him? For a moment, as their lips had touched, she'd thought she'd made a chink in that huge wall he had round himself. *Wrong*.

But he'd done the right thing by calling a halt. They'd been on a course headed for disaster. And, ridiculously, recklessly, she hadn't cared. She'd been spurred on by the thrill of the baby, the excitement of the quiz night. His touch.

Her heart stalled. The quiz. She hadn't told him the result. He'd need to know, and what it involved. *Later*. If later ever came.

'Skye. Hi. Reporting for duty.' Adam bustled in with a wheelchair and flicked an easy salute.

She scanned his face for anything other than a normal professional response to seeing her again and found nothing. He seemed focused, though. Clearly he didn't have a whirlwind blowing through his stomach. 'Where's the patient?'

'Room Two. But wait, I'll give you a quick handover out here. He's not keen on going anywhere, but he's got ST elevations. Chest pain. Blood pressure a bit high at one sixty over ninety. He's had a couple of squirts of GTN, aspirin and morphine. That helped the pain, but now he thinks he's invincible. Hence the refusal to budge.' She handed Adam a summary page and tried to focus on the information and not his blue eyes, interesting face or the weird one-sided chemistry she had buzzing through her. 'Needs a cardiac opinion stat. Oh, and we put a line in for IV access.'

'Okay. Let's get on with it.' He nodded and wandered through to Room Two, leaving Skye lost for words. No mention of the other night, no soft look, nothing between them, apart from her red cheeks. He'd treated her like he would treat anyone else, not someone with whom he'd shared a mind-blowing kiss.

Just like Brian had when they'd been in front of his

other students, her friends, anyone. Like she wasn't important. Looking back, she couldn't believe she'd allowed him to do that, but in the blush of first love and her immature need to be needed she'd let him run roughshod over her.

And now, heck, they had an emergency and Adam was right to focus on the patient. 'Hello, sir. My name's Adam and I'm lucky enough to be escorting you to Auckland General.'

Skye squeezed into the tiny consult room, refusing to inhale the delicious smell that had breezed in with Adam, and unhooked their patient from the ECG machine. 'This is Eric Bailey. Woke with chest pains earlier. His ECG's a bit wobbly and Connor thinks a visit to the cardiac unit would be good. Isn't that right, Eric?'

The old man scowled and shifted his oxygen mask to speak. 'Too much fuss, just indigestion. It's just a niggle.'

'Well, let's be on the safe side.' Adam offered the man his arm. 'I need you to sit on this chair for me. Do you think you could slide on over?'

Eric folded his arms over his ample abdomen. 'I'm not going.'

Why did every man she met have to be so darned stubborn? Skye interjected, 'You need to be checked out. It's for the best, Eric.'

'For you perhaps. Gets me out of your hair. But I don't want to go. There's things need doing. I'm behind schedule.'

'Me too.' Skye glanced at the wall clock. Time was of the essence, but spooking Eric would only make the old man dig his great muddy boots in further. She looked at Adam and silently asked him to support her. He nodded his assent, his gaze flitting over to the flapping ECG leads as if he wished he could put them back on again.

He straightened, towering over them all, and looked

Eric straight in the eye. 'Mr Bailey, what line of work are you in?'

'Farming. Dairy.'

Adam nodded. 'You have a tractor?'

'Naturally.'

'And what do you do if it breaks down?'

'Give it a kick.' Eric had a glimmer of mischief in his rheumy eyes.

Adam bit his cheek. 'And then?'

'What's this got to do with e-chi-cees and cardy-somethings? You're all talking in a foreign language.'

'I try to be a plain speaker, like you, Mr Bailey. I don't like fuss.' Adam paused, obviously trying to find the right words. His voice deepened, but was calm and clear. He didn't invite question and imbued just enough authority to make anyone do what he asked. Army training, she guessed.

And again, for no rational reason, she wanted to know more about him, his background. What made him so wary, and after his brush-off the other night, why the heck did she care?

She needed to give him a wide berth, and perhaps a kick up the backside for being so rude.

As he spoke he guided Eric to sit upright and put his feet flat on the floor, giving the old guy no chance to argue. 'Sometimes us medics can fancy things up, use words you don't understand, makes you confused, right?'

'Yes.'

'And I hate being confused. Not knowing what's happening. I like honesty.' He paused and caught Skye's eye. She thought for a moment that he was trying to tell her something but he quickly turned back to Eric. 'I won't give you any rubbish. Think of your heart as your engine. It's got a rattle, so it needs a check-up. I can't say exactly what's wrong, but leave it too long and who knows what'll happen?'

'You think I should go to the hospital?'

'What have you got to lose? You'll be back home soon enough.'

'What if I've blown a gasket and I don't come home at all?' And there it was—the old man was scared.

Adam's stance softened. He crouched down to Eric, put a hand on his shoulder, in a gesture of solidarity rather than pity. Skye heaved out a breath. Adam knew exactly how to approach this. No jokes, no pointless chatter, like she did. Just honest-to-goodness straight talking. 'As you know, a gasket is fixable. Same with hearts, if we get to the problem in time. There are tests that work out what's wrong and the docs fix it. Soon as you know it, you'll be fit as a fiddle.'

'Ach, you've got an answer for everything.'

'I try.'

'Okay. Let's go.' Eric nodded, winced and slumped back in the chair. Skye began to wheel it to the front door. No way was she taking a risk on him changing his mind.

Dan appeared, breathless, from the reception area. 'Sorry, I got waylaid. Just got the lowdown from Connor. I thought he'd be on paternity leave?'

Another stubborn man. 'He's supposed to be, but he keeps coming in. Checking on things, me, the clinic, the locum.'

Adam's lips curled up to the side as he nodded to his partner then loaded their patient into the van. Damn him, he could dredge up a smile for Dan and comfort for Eric. But not even a glimmer of warmth for her. He jumped down from the van and approached Dan. 'Well, we managed just fine without you.'

'Give it up. Skye's the only one around here who's irreplaceable.' Dan slapped Adam on the back. 'Now, Connor told me about the quiz-night win. Well done, you two.'

Adam stilled for a second, his eyes wide and chest puffed out. 'We won?'

Skye pursed her lips and tried not to gloat. 'Yes. We did. Nine-week winning streak. Thanks for your help.'

'What did we win?'

'One hundred dollars behind the bar, which we usually share with the rest of the crowd. Oh...' *Now for the real doozy.* She added a tinge of nonchalance to her voice. Had no intention of showing him what she felt about their joint prize. 'And a bonus balloon ride for two. Connor can't make it, so I guess it's you and me. Saturday morning if the weather's right. Something to do with being dependent on thermals.'

Dan grinned. 'Lucky. I've always wanted to do that.'

'You can take my place if you want.' Adam's face darkened, his jaw tightened. He looked every bit as if a balloon ride at dawn with a woman he had recently kissed was the last thing on earth he would contemplate doing. And he wasn't making an effort to hide his discomfort.

Irritation rushed through her. That was it. The final nail.

She wasn't going to be sucked in to working out what was going on in his head. She'd had her fill of insecurity, she needed to put the kiss behind her and move on. Quickly. 'Yes, Dan. Why don't you come? It'll be awesome. A nice way to say goodbye to my home, floating off into the clouds.'

Dan shook his head. 'I've got an extra shift on Saturday. Need the cash, sorry. Looks like you'll have to go, mate.'

Adam turned away, didn't deign to acknowledge Dan's words with a comment.

Trying to save further embarrassment all round, Skye spoke through her tight throat. Bad enough to be blown

off, but in front of a friend too? That hurt. 'No. It's okay.
I'll find someone else. See you.'

She stepped back and walked towards the surgery door,
trying to control her chagrin but nagged by a strange feeling of being watched. As she reached the threshold she
turned back to check, and smacked into Adam's hard ribcage.

'Oh.' Jumping back didn't erase the fact she'd touched
him again. Felt his heat. Tension and desire spread through
her. 'I thought you'd gone.' *Hoped* you'd gone.

'Clearly not.' He shrugged. 'What time do you need
to be there?'

'Where?'

He rubbed a hand over his jaw. 'The balloon place.'

'Six thirty.'

'Okay.' Sucking in a deep breath he nodded. 'I can do
that.'

'Has Dan put you up to this? You don't have to. You
don't owe me anything.' *Definitely not the dregs of your
pity.*

'I know.'

'Please don't bother yourself. I will find someone else.
I have other friends.'

'Skye. Stop and listen to me.' He touched her arm and
looked as if he was trying to convince himself as much as
her. 'No arguments. I'll pick you up at six.'

CHAPTER SIX

You are out of your mind.

Clearly. Adam slumped in his truck and rested his head on the steering-wheel.

This is the very last time you do anything for a woman. Guilt or no guilt.

He tried to control his raging tachycardia. He'd done some damn-fool things in his life—crazy ops in the middle of enemy territory, casevacs under fire—but none had felt as mad as a balloon ride over amazing countryside with a beautiful woman. Any other man would kill for the chance. How the hell he'd convince her to go up on her own he didn't know. But that was Plan A.

He huffed out a shallow breath and almost laughed. Spooked by an inflatable. At least he could see the funny side, even though it didn't change the way he felt. Incredible, how a single moment in his life had changed everything—his friends, his marriage, his outlook. But, damn, he would not let it beat him.

'Good morning.' Skye, fresh faced and make-up free, climbed into the passenger seat. Her smile was on full megawatt, with that kid-on-Christmas-Eve look again.

'Hi. All set?'

'Oh, yes. I'm so excited.' Without her usual dark eye-liner her eyes shone clear and bright. Breathtaking—if his breath hadn't already been sucked out of him by good old-fashioned fear.

But he'd committed to not spoiling Skye's day. He owed her, to deliver her to the take-off zone anyway. His mood hadn't exactly been welcoming last time he'd seen her. The truth was, the kiss bothered him. The way they'd parted bothered him. Skye bothered him. In ways he hadn't imagined possible. Dodging bullets was easier than dealing with this.

She dropped her bag onto the floor as she fastened her safety belt. She had a black woollen beanie pulled over her ears. A tight black merino jumper hugged her curves. Black skinny jeans reached down to black canvas trainers. She looked like a pint-sized assassin or a cat burglar. A grinning cat burglar. 'I've never done anything like this before. I've got the map and the instructions.'

'Let's get going, then. You nav, I'll drive.' He hoped she didn't notice the shake in his hand.

Leaving the coast behind them, Adam concentrated on the unfamiliar route meandering westwards through wiggly roads flanked by dense bush. The tarmac gradually gave way to a narrow gravel track that climbed steadily out of the trees and into high country shrouded in the first tentative fingers of pink daylight.

Patchwork fields stretched out before them, and around them nothing stirred. It was like the whole world was asleep, at peace. He could get used to living here.

'I wonder what it's like? Do you think there'll be a jolt on lift-off? Will I get airsick?' She laughed, breaking the silence. Her voice cracked a little, with forced jollity. Excitement or nerves? He hoped to God her nerves weren't because of him. He hadn't meant to get involved at any level but the spectre of their kiss hung around like a damp shroud, colouring every word. It would be better when she left and he could relax into his new life of peace. *Peace. Yeah, right.* 'Is it going to be cold up there?'

'I don't know, Skye.' He didn't want to imagine what it would be like scudding the clouds without a 'chute. He'd lost count of the number of times he'd flown. But not once had he done it in a picnic basket with delusions of grandeur. 'I've never been in a balloon before. I'm sure they'll brief us.'

'Sorry, I know. *Too many questions.* I have a habit of chattering when I'm excited. Brian used to hate it…'

'Brian?' His interest was piqued. He glanced over to look at her.

'My ex.' She chewed her bottom lip and gave him a brief grin. Shook her head. 'Never mind.'

'Recent ex?' The guy Dan had mentioned? The one that had made her swear off men?

'A couple of years ago, when I came back here to look after Mum, things kind of ended.'

'Kind of?' Did she still have the hots for him?

'No, really. Ended. He couldn't come and visit. I couldn't go there. He got miffed. We argued a lot. It wasn't pretty.' She pointed to a left turn. 'Up there, through the gate.'

'He wanted you to stay in Auckland?'

'We'd been together two years. It was easier, he said, if I stayed in the city. But I couldn't. He wanted me to choose between him and my dying mother.' She smiled, but this time it was backlit with hurt. 'When he didn't call I thought he was being enigmatic. He made so many promises to come out and reneged on every one. I thought he was just busy, I made excuses for him. I didn't like to pressure him.'

'That'd be you through and through.' Never making any demands on anyone, always putting herself at the back of the line. He steered his truck through a farm gate and down to a wide field, wishing they hadn't arrived quite so soon.

'Turns out he couldn't visit because he couldn't get time off from his *wife*.' Bitterness leached through her words.

'Wife?' Adam pulled up in a muddy makeshift parking area and braked sharply. Dawn light filtered through the mud-splattered windshield, illuminating her face. Which resembled beetroot.

He bit back a bitter laugh. She'd clearly unwittingly overstepped her own boundaries with this Brian joker. He couldn't imagine sunny Skye ever doing anything to wilfully hurt someone else. She clutched her bag against her chest like a shield. How could he be shocked? She'd been hurt, played for a fool. That had to bite deep. 'He was married? You were someone's mistress?'

Horror lit her eyes. 'Turns out I didn't know anything about him really. Everything he told me from day one was a lie. He didn't wear a ring. Never mentioned anything about being married. How would I know? Two whole years of my life wasted. I believed him. I wanted to believe him.' She dug him in the ribs with her finger and flashed him that cheerful smile that lit up everyone's day. 'Quit laughing at me.'

'I thought you liked it when I laughed.' Hell, *he* liked it when he laughed. It was just that he only seemed to do it when Skye was around. It was infectious too, Adam realised, as his mouth contorted into an unfamiliar shape.

'I do. You look different when you smile.'

The heat in the car notched up a few degrees. Something ephemeral simmered between them. The kiss. The touch of her fingers against his ribs. Her opening up about her life. Telling him her secrets.

Don't get too cosy. This whole venture had been a mistake. He should have decided to keep his distance, not spend more time in a confined space with her. Especially when she looked at him with those huge sad eyes that threatened to send him to the far side.

He flicked on the air-con and checked the digital clock on the dash. 'Looks like we're early.'

'He said to wait here and he'd come and get us.'

Adam drummed his fingers on the steering-wheel, trying to think of a different line of conversation. But curiosity got the better of him. He leaned back in his chair, shifted to face her. 'So, now we have a few minutes to kill, tell me more about your wild mistressing days.'

'As soon as I found out he was married I ended it.' She laughed, her shoulders relaxing. 'He wasn't expecting that. Thought I'd follow him to the ends of the earth. He was sorely mistaken.'

'Good for you. I like your spirit. Messy?'

'And then some. If you imagine a relationship being like my kitchen table…messy, cluttered, grubby. Brian could do a lot of sweet-talking, but his actions didn't amount to much. After we broke up I discovered I wasn't his first extra-marital and I don't think I'll be the last.'

'He sounds like one hell of a guy. You're better off without men like that.'

'Ones that play games? Tell lies? Sure. Don't I know it.' He got the feeling there was a lot more to this story than she let on. She peered at him through the half-light. 'Now, your turn, seeing as we're divulging dirty little secrets. Girlfriend? Wife? Any horror stories? Gory details?'

Don't even go there. 'One wife. Divorced. Long story.' More collateral damage from the chopper attack. Tempting though it was to share his story with Skye, his life wasn't for public consumption. He didn't want to revisit the past, the reasons his marriage had failed. He had enough to think about right now, without soiling the day further.

A glare of headlights made them turn and watch as a

four-wheel drive pulled into the field. *Great timing.* Out of one difficult situation into another. His blood flowed cold. 'Okay, here we go.'

'What are you waiting for? Jump in, quick!' Skye reached over the basket and gripped Adam's wrist. Panic flooded through her. *Why was he standing frozen like that?* Five heads turned and watched as she tried to pull him into the basket. She flashed the pilot and the other passengers a quick smile. 'Just wait a second.'

All through the briefing Adam had stayed strangely silent, kept himself at a distance from the rest of the group. Same when they'd inflated the balloon with the large hairdryer fan thing. He'd stood back and watched. She shook his arm. 'Come on, slowcoach, we're taking off.'

His hand, ice cold, tightened around hers and he fixed her with his gaze. Dark clouds flashed across his eyes, which he masked with a determined glare. 'I—'

The pilot gunned hot air into the gold and black silk, a roar filled her ears and obliterated Adam's words.

'Is it your leg? Can't you climb in?' But she knew it wasn't that. In her dealings with Adam he had never once complained about the limp in his gait or pain she knew he must have. Few people limped without soreness. She'd seen him power down a beach, lift fourteen-stone patients. It wasn't the leg wound stopping him getting into the balloon, it was something else. But he was too darned proud to admit it.

A roaring inside her head clashed with the noisy burners. Had he only agreed to this for her? He'd offered the ride to Dan first, but she'd thought it was a get-out grab. That he didn't want to spend time with her.

But…what if there were other reasons? She'd rabbited on and never once asked if he was happy to come. And he'd agreed, even though something spooked him about this flight. He'd agreed to do this for her.

Adam might not be all fancy words like Brian. He might struggle with intimacy. But his actions meant more than anything. That thought confused her, worried her. Excited her.

She needed to give him an out. 'If you want to stay here...'

'What? No. I'm fine.' He obviously wasn't fine by a long shot but his voice carried a steel she hadn't ever heard from him before. He paused and closed his eyes. Muttered something under his breath that sounded Latin. *Semper* something. Then, determination in his jaw and rippling through every sinew, he gulped oxygen and catapulted into the basket.

Skye peered up at him as he found his feet and squeezed into the huddle. His bulky frame dominated the small space. A tight frown etched across his forehead but he nodded slowly, unclenched his fists. So many questions hurtled round her brain. The main one being, *What happened to you?*

Every minute she spent with him his complexity deepened, along with her worrying need to get to know him better. 'Are you okay?'

'Of course.' He turned away from her and she decided not to push him further. She'd probably already overstepped the mark. If he needed to vent his problems, he would.

A huge blast of hot air distracted her and without warning, no jolt, no big fuss, they glided into the air. The farm buildings below became toy-sized. The animals lazing in the early hazy sunshine looked like miniatures compared to the huge black shadow scudding across their pasture. 'Wow. Just look at that.'

A tight knot formed in her chest as she looked down at the landscape of her birth. Majestic rugged hilltops covered in dense native bush gave way to swathes of golden sands, deserted horseshoe bays and lush silver ocean.

Many times she'd stopped on the beach to watch a pod of dolphins playing, or orca whales on their journey to a morning feed. Weekends and holidays had been spent fishing off those bays or visiting the many tiny islands dotted around the gulf, witnessing tiny blue penguins take a first swim. As the sun glinted off the water she traced a wave back to shore, then her gaze moved to the palm-tree-lined roads, the farms dotted along the hillsides. Endless green. Paradise.

The knot tightened. Floating through a serene sky may have been a fitting way to say goodbye to her home town, but until now she'd grown blasé at its startling beauty, at what she was leaving behind. Too busy planning her trip and what she'd do away from Atanga Bay, she hadn't had time to think about leaving the physical splendour. For the first time she realised she'd miss this special place. 'It's so beautiful, I guess I'd got too used to it. But from up here it's amazing.'

Next to her Adam bristled but didn't answer, his hands clutching the basket ridge as he stared straight ahead.

She touched his shoulder and gained his attention. 'You having fun?'

'Sure.' *Liar.* That was about all he could muster for a reply. Adam hauled in air and waited for the adrenalin surge to slow. Tachycardia threatened.

Stupid for looking such a damned fool, letting his past tangle with Skye's special day. Her hand fitted into his tight fist. For a moment he relished the human contact, grateful she didn't pry any further, the simple intimacy of holding hands much more than the kiss they'd shared.

It said, *I care*, plain and simple. And he held on to that thought as the trees slipped below them.

They floated out towards the sea, skimming over cornfields and a pewter road winding down to the almost-white stretch of sand. Adam's eyes snapped shut as he counted to ten. He could not let Skye—anyone—see him at his weakest. *Always calm*.

'From here you can see a panorama of the east coast and Northland region. To the left we have the bush hills of Brynderwyn.' The pilot's voice made Adam jump out of his daydream. *Nightmare*. 'To the right directly below us we have Atanga Bay and to the south the communities of Leigh and Mangawhai. Northwards we have Whangarei, Russell, Ninety-Mile Beach and then a whole lot of nothing.'

'Look! Look! There's my house! The black roof. Oh. There's no one there. The boys promised they'd get up to wave.' Skye gripped his hand more tightly, her voice laced with disappointment. 'Should have known better.'

He willed his eyes to open. Hoping the nausea and the dizziness would stop. 'Maybe they didn't realise the time.'

'Maybe they just don't care.'

'Sure they do, they just have trouble showing it.'

'You can say that again.' It wasn't like Skye to frown. His free hand fisted. Hell, her brothers needed a good dressing down. After all she did for them, what she'd given up. If only they knew how much their inaction hurt her.

But speaking out against them would make him the outsider. From what he knew of Skye so far, loyalty to her kin ran very deep.

'Oh, there's the medical centre. The pub. A few waving there.' She dropped his hand and waved frantically. 'Hi! Hi!' Her words lost on the wind.

Adam peered through one half-open eye over the top of

the basket, which, ridiculously, only reached to his waist. Way down below he glimpsed the craggy hills and wide expanse of ocean. A swathe of sand dunes delineated the beach.

His stomach whirled and he had the distinct feeling of falling. A video played in his head. So much air. Too much metal. Pain. Dead eyes staring up at him. His heart thumped. He closed his eyes again and willed the damned ride to finish.

'My head's hot,' Skye whispered as her hand squeezed his again. 'How's yours?'

'Okay.' He forced words through clenched teeth then opened his eyes to see her face inches from him, anchoring him. 'It's the burner, it makes everything hot. Maybe you should take the woolly hat off?'

'Can't possibly.' She shrugged. 'Hat hair.'

'Don't be silly. You'll be fine. Who cares? You always look great.'

'No, I don't.' She wiped a hand across her stomach and looked at him as if his words were a foreign language. Or lies. 'It's okay, I know you're just being nice. You don't have to do or say anything just to make me feel better. In fact, I'd prefer honesty straight down the line.'

Anger mixed with the churning in his guts. He gripped the rough edge of the wicker. 'He did a real number on you, eh?'

'Who?

'That Brian jerk.'

'I guess.' Her cheeks burned red as she turned away. 'Don't ruin a beautiful day.'

Immediately regretting his reference to her ex, he tried for lightness. She was right. Reading between her lines, she'd been through enough. 'Come here. Don't be silly. You'll get too hot.'

He grabbed for the hat but the basket lurched under him. Panic gripped his stomach. He fought it. 'God. No.'

Bile rose in his throat and the bitter taste of acid filled his mouth. Flashes of light filled his vision. He needed to get off, feel solid ground under his feet. He would never do this again. Never. He couldn't do flying. He couldn't do playful. He'd do well to remember that.

'Adam? Adam? Look at me.' Skye's lips were close to his and he realised he'd slunk down the side of the basket and was crouching on his haunches. Her blurred face swam in and out of focus.

'I'm okay. Fine.'

'I know you are.' She breathed into his ear, her words a salve to his racing heart rate. 'We're starting to go down now. So how about you concentrate on this instead?'

She placed a hand on his cheek, her soft fingertips stroking the unscarred side of his face. Her eyes burned into his with a blatant message of desire.

That simmering connection buzzed between them again. Focusing on her face took some of the terror away. Before he could open his mouth to speak, her soft lips pressed against his. A sweet kiss, an affirmation, kindness. Not what he'd expected. Or should even think about. But exactly what he needed. And she knew it too.

The invisible threads between them tightened and entwined whenever he was with her. And, hell, he should be careful of that. Knew they were heading for uncharted territory. But in the midst of the chaos inside him she held him steady.

He hauled her against his chest and squeezed her close, his fingers running over the weird woolly beanie that remained firmly stuck to her head. Holding her was wrong, he couldn't take this anywhere, but it was all kinds of right too.

A snatched moment in the middle of a crisis, an anchor, a release. That's all. They could both walk away afterwards.

The kiss ended almost as soon as it had begun. She pulled away and wriggled her nose. 'Stand up, have one last try. You'll regret it if you don't.'

'Honey, there are lots of things I'll regret, and watching the earth rush up to meet me in a picnic basket isn't one of them.' But he took her hand and slowly stood, urged on by her touch.

Suddenly they were descending at speed.

'Whoa… Holy… Watch it. Too fast. Too fast. More height, now,' he yelled at the pilot as the balloon jerked. Branches and treetops loomed close enough to touch, then… 'Duck! Everyone, brace.'

He squished Skye under his shoulder, battered the kauri branches out of the way. His only thought was to protect her, keep her safe. Every muscle braced against the corner of the basket. 'Don't worry. Hold on to me. We'll be fine.'

'I know. But I'll stay here like this if you don't mind.' He felt her smile against his chest. That alone empowered him.

Then with a whoosh and a roar they skimmed upwards away from the danger. Adam pushed out a breath, but kept his hold on Skye. Just in case, right?

The pilot grinned. 'Everyone okay? Sorry about that. Wind shear can happen sometimes. All under control.'

'Thanks for the warning, pal.' Adam released his grip on Skye and checked her over.

'Stop fussing. I'm fine.' Her face crumpled a little as she surveyed him. 'But you have a scratch along your sca—'

'Never mind me.' He swiped a hand across his cheek. Felt the rough edges of his gouged skin. Wet. Only now did it start to sting. 'I've had a lot worse.'

'But you're bleeding.' She reached into her bag and brought out a paper tissue. 'Here, hold this against it.'

'There's that mothering thing again.'

'Like you'd let me.'

But he kind of liked it. Liked it that she wanted to take care of him. Even if it did make him feel like a wuss. A cared-for wuss. Did that make him weak? Weak and on edge. There was a heady combination. The day could only get better.

'I'll do it.' He grabbed the tissue and held it against his scar. 'Everyone else okay?'

The young couple next to them, pale but smiling, gave him a thumbs-up. The two elderly sisters broke their chatter to nod.

And the pilot beamed back. 'Not a scratch, apart from you, buddy. The chase crew has a first-aid kit. I'll get them to take a look.'

He spoke into a crackly walkie-talkie, waited for an affirmative response, then spoke to them all, pointing to a large field up ahead. 'Looks like a good place to land. Hold on.'

To their left a four-wheel drive sped along a winding road that grew larger and larger as they descended. The world righted itself, oxygen filled Adam's lungs, deeper now, and the adrenalin flow slowed. *Finally*.

'Watch out, a little bump coming,' the pilot yelled as they shuddered and bumped across furrows that pocked the mud.

'Little bump?' Skye clung to Adam and chuckled as they skidded to a halt, aided by the chase crew securing ropes.

For the last few minutes the feel of her had been the only thing keeping him sane. Stupid as it was, he didn't want to let go. 'That's as euphemistic as one of our *little scratch* reassurances when we're about to give an injection. Come on, let's get out. There's a champagne break-fast with our name on it waiting at the Old Bank Hotel.'

'Race you.' Not needing an excuse, he jumped out of the basket, his ankle jolting at the first touch of solid ground. A sharp stab fingered through his nerve pathways, an electric current of pain shuddering through his leg. He tried to cover his wince. *Damn, not again.* When would his body stop working against him?

Stomping down into thick mud, he steadied himself, worked his foot in a normal rotation, eased out the ache and held his hands out to catch Skye. He shoved his pain aside and focused on her, the feel of her gone for too long already.

'Hey, what about me?' One of the elderly sisters reached out for his hand, a cheeky glint in her pale blue eyes. 'Don't we all get a lift?'

'At your service, ma'am. Give me a moment.' Reluctantly he lowered Skye to the ground, skimming his hands over her butt, waist and shoulders. He wondered what she looked like under those clothes. She felt so good, warm, real. He imagined the smooth silk of her skin under his touch, the caress of flesh against flesh.

Not that it was any of his business to wonder.

Then he helped first one, then both ladies out of the basket. 'Watch your step now, it's a bit boggy.'

Biting back the pain radiating up his leg, he turned to catch up with Skye. A scream from behind had him twisting back round. One of the sisters lay on the floor in a heap, her face screwed up in agony. 'Ooh. Help! My ankle. I've hurt my ankle.'

You and me both. 'Can I take a look?' But he didn't wait for her answer. Pulling up her trouser leg, he gently lifted off her shoe and sock and surveyed the damage. 'Swelling already. Does it hurt here?'

'Yes. Yes.' She squeezed her eyes closed as he pressed against her rapidly swelling flesh. Either she had a low pain threshold or she'd done serious damage. He helped her to stand. 'Can you put any weight on it?'

She tentatively put her foot on the ground. 'No. I'm sorry. I can hop.'

Making a seventy-odd-year-old woman hop? Never. 'I think we'll do this the old-fashioned way.' He swooped her up into his arms. 'Comfy?'

'Ooh, yes.' She put thin arms round his neck. 'It's worth the pain just for this.'

'We need to get you out of all this mud and to an X-ray facility.' He looked over to Skye, who had kept back and allowed him to reframe himself as a medic. Not vulnerable. Just what he needed. Pain and fear diminished a man, but saving someone—that was where pride and honour lay.

She leaned against the bonnet of the chase-crew vehicle and waved him over. Even from this distance her sunny smile lit her face, that weird hat still covering her jet-black hair. Awareness spiked through the heat surging through his stomach. He shouldn't be feeling like this. Not wanting a woman so much he hurt. He should stop things before he got in over his head. He couldn't give her what she needed. Hell, he couldn't give her a great deal of anything.

Then he set about walking towards her. Every uneven step fired shards of pain through his ankle. But that was nothing compared to the burning realisation that he was already in way too deep.

CHAPTER SEVEN

'I LOVE this tradition of always having champagne after a balloon flight. It was amazing, seeing my home town look like a street of play houses. So beautiful too, seeing the landscape on such a huge scale.' It had been a stark realisation that she'd be sad to leave the place. Skye raised her flute of champagne and held it out to Adam's glass. The rest of the crowd had gone out to the sun garden, leaving her alone with him in the hotel's tiny lounge area. Which was a good thing. And bad too.

Watching him grapple with whatever demon he'd faced in that balloon had raised him incredibly high in her estimation of him. That stubborn streak of his, the one that wouldn't let him wallow in his fear, made him more of a man.

As she'd watched him hobble across that pocked field with Annabel in his arms, his hotness rating had notched up into the danger zone too. Who wouldn't find a rescuer attractive? The tummy flutters she had every time she looked at him were just a normal healthy reaction to a good-looking man. 'Here's to the best balloon ride ever. And a very scrummy-looking breakfast.'

'Mine looks great, but yours is far too healthy.'

'But slimming.' She nodded at his glass. 'Er...our toast?'

'Oh. Yes. To my first and last balloon ride *ever*.' He mustered a small smile and clinked his glass to hers, his voice gruff and deep. 'I can drink champagne any time.'

'Then you should. I adore it. Especially at eight o'clock in the morning.' She took a sip, feeling sinfully decadent. 'I'm going to drink it in France, Italy, Greece, Germany. Whenever I can.'

'Please tell me you're not thinking of taking a balloon ride in every country too?'

'No. I couldn't afford it, for a start. But it wouldn't be the same…' *Without you*, she nearly said. And wondered where the heck they were going.

Two kisses, cuddles, a physical closeness that neither appeared to be able to deny. And yet he kept himself so walled up that cracking his hard veneer would take a lot longer than she had. She didn't even know if she wanted to try. In less than three weeks she'd be gone, his face and story part of a different chapter of her life.

She looked down at her plate of mixed fruits and yoghurt. Suddenly her appetite, normally too healthy, had disappeared into the vortex swirling in her stomach. Not even his bacon and eggs appealed. 'It was great of the chase crew to take Annabel to that new X-ray facility. We can enjoy our bubbles knowing her ankle's being well cared for. Sometimes we carers need a pep-up too.' She drew a breath. 'When I looked after Mum it seemed like an endless draw on my resources. What's it like, being an army medic? You must have seen some terrible things. You get debriefed, I guess?'

She hoped she wasn't being too obvious by steering the conversation down this path. Hoped, too, that by admitting she'd needed something he might join in and start to open up too. Negotiating with her brothers through difficult years had taught her that asking a man outright about his pain only sent him scuttling back into his shell.

His shoulders dropped and he looked like he was making a conscious effort to relax. After a mouthful of organic cured ham and free-range yolk he spoke. 'It was grim at times. But we got what we needed.'

'Like?'

'Time out, leave. Debriefing, psych help.' A shoulder lifted. 'The usual.'

'I don't know what usual is for a soldier.'

He shrugged and put down his knife and fork. She got the feeling she'd overstepped the mark. How did she have such strong feelings for someone who refused to let her in?

But he swallowed and continued, 'Sorry. I'm not used to talking about my former life.'

'Ooh? Was it hush-hush?' She tapped the side of her nose. Trying to make light of it. 'Top secret—*if I tell you I'll have to kill you* kind of stuff?'

'Oh, yes.' He leaned closer and finally managed a small smile, making her thoughts scatter. 'Very secret.'

'I have ways of making you talk.'

'I bet you do. If I could get a word in. Some skill you've got there, grinning people to death. The army could do with a weapon like that.' He slugged the last of his drink. 'But I'm highly trained and immune. Nothing you could do would make me give up secrets. Well, almost nothing…'

'Oh?' Her heart jittered at his closeness. Heat washed over her skin.

He moved to the edge of his seat, closed the space between them even more and lowered his voice. 'Shame on you, Skye with an "e". Wanting me to spill government secrets. They'll have me locked up. Or shot at dawn.'

'Which would be a terrible shame.'

'Yes, it would.' His breath whispered over her as he

spoke. That invisible thread yanked tight, a force that she needed to resist. Being this close to him made her body want things she shouldn't want. She tipped her throat back to get out of his space, took a sip of fizz, caught an errant drop with her tongue. 'Oops.'

'Let me get that for you.' His eyes slid from her mouth to the glass and back again. He grabbed a napkin and dabbed her chin. She tried not to look at him.

Wafting a beer mat in front of her hot face, she controlled her ragged breathing. 'Thanks, soldier boy.'

Oh, hell. To her horror she was giving off all the wrong signals. She hardly recognised her own voice. It was hoarse and husky, and had dropped an octave in response to his proximity, to his smell. *To him.*

'So tell me about the nose ring.' His hand cupped her face as he turned her cheek to get a better look at the diamond.

The sensation of his skin against hers sent ripples of desire skittering through her stomach. 'That came out of nowhere.'

He ran his thumb across the stud. 'I was just looking and got to wondering...'

She moved away from his hand, managed a mouthful of strawberry. 'It was a present, from me to me.'

'For what?'

Surviving. 'It was the first page in my new chapter. Doing something for me. Being who I am. Skye Williams. I tried too hard to be something everyone else wanted me to be.' Brian. Her stepdad. And she'd failed at every level, in their eyes anyway. 'I liked the idea of being a bit different. Most people think it's too *out there*. Same with the black clothes. People are always trying to get me to dress in colours. You wouldn't believe how many bright scarves I get for Christmas. I like black, it's comfortable. It's me.'

And it hid a multitude of sins. Things Brian had poked fun at; her larger-than-he-liked love handles, the curve of her stomach, wobbly thighs. Things he'd wanted her to change, had forced her to hate.

Adam nodded. 'In the army we were told when to eat, when to pee, what to think. It was hard to express any kind of uniqueness. They don't like it, don't want it. It's not encouraged.'

She imagined a whole platoon of Adams. An army of loyal hard men who conquered every fear, every enemy. Men who were brave and strong and sinfully sexy. The thought thrilled her. 'Is that why you got the dragonfly tattoo? To make you different underneath your uniform?'

'*No.*' He knew his voice was sharp. He hadn't meant it to be. She jumped away.

His hand darted to his chest. The tattoo wasn't to make him different. It was to make him belong. To a group of guys worth more than the army put together, than the whole darned defence force. Men he'd have willingly laid down his life for. If they were still alive. It was soppy, they'd all known it, but they'd had their own band of brothers. 'It's a long story.'

'It's okay.' She laid her hand on his. 'Any time you want to talk, feel free. Sometimes it's good to share stuff.'

'It's better left alone.' Although it was tempting to share, for the first time ever. But, then, where would he be? He didn't want to open wounds again. His eyebrows rose. 'I don't think I've ever met anyone quite so forthright as you.'

'So you don't speak your mind in the army either? All that training taught you to button up?' She frowned. 'Yeah, great approach. Keep it all bottled up until you feel like you're going to explode. I've been there. It works real well too. Until you go crazy.'

She was playing a double bluff. And it was working.

The coy smile in her eyes told him she wouldn't judge, and he wanted to believe it. Maybe he should just tell her enough to let some of the pressure escape for a while. He opened his mouth to start, but she got there before him.

'Adam, I know something spooked you earlier.'

'Oh?'

'You were scared.'

'Like hell I was.'

'Yes, you were, and that's nothing to be ashamed of. Whatever it was that made you hesitate, you conquered it.'

He'd got into the balloon. Big deal. Although the tachycardia still hadn't quite resolved. 'Don't mother me.'

'Sorry.' She snatched her hand away, obviously stung by his words. He wanted to take them back. But they were out there. Damn, she had him tongue-tied. One minute he was kissing her, the next he was seriously offending her. He needed space to work out what he wanted. What she needed. It certainly wasn't him.

'I'm not trying to mother you. I'm trying to understand.' Pain flitted over her eyes. 'I thought we had something going here? We seem to have a connection. Or am I blind? And now stupid?'

'No...'

She stood and gave him a wobbly smile. 'Forget it. I'll get the bill.'

'Skye. Wait.'

But she'd made her way to the counter. Couldn't even wait for the waitress to bring the bill over.

He followed her, ignoring the pain vibrating through his foot. Pushed a fifty over and walked out to the truck. She stood at the passenger door, waiting for him to open it. 'Is your leg sore?'

'No.'

'Are you sure? Just you seem to be in pain.'

'I'm fine. Really.' He'd done some damage but he wasn't going to admit it. He'd get it checked out. Later.

Right now he was torn between keeping his private memories to himself and making inroads into the mess he'd created with this beautiful woman. The beautiful woman won. 'Skye. A lot of stuff happened. Some friends died. I got injured, a medical discharge and a whole lot of fallout. I don't talk about it. Okay?'

'It might help.'

'I'm through with talking. Now I need to move on. That's why I'm here. A new start, a job I love in a place I like.' He scraped in a breath and leaned next to her against the truck door. Glad of a chance to make amends, a little anyway. 'I was a mess for a while but now I'm sorting myself out. That's why I've got to make a go of things here. To prove I can.'

She hugged her arms over her jumper, the tension evaporating from her taut stance. He got the feeling she'd done a lot of forgiving over the years, a lot of understanding.

There was something in her that made him want to talk. She nodded thoughtfully, that strange woollen hat still covering her head. 'And I'm pushing you too hard. I can't imagine what active combat is like, and I don't want to force you into telling me.'

'You have a right to know why I don't share things.' This was the first time in a long time he'd even wanted to open up. 'I want to forget all that happened. I lost too much.'

'Your wife?'

'Yes.'

Her eyes widened. 'I can't imagine you married.'

He felt the smile flicker over his lips. 'That hard to believe, huh? Skye, I wasn't always like this.'

'I know. I get glimpses of a different man sometimes.

One who trusts and believes. One who smiles, and kisses like a devil. But then you shut up shop. I wish we'd had a chance.'

She palmed his scar. Something his wife had never been able to do. The simple act almost undid him. All he wanted was to hold her. His resolve crashed and burnt on the car-park gravel.

He pulled her close, gave in to temptation and nibbled on her bottom lip. She tasted of strawberry yoghurt and sunshine, and every part of him ached to taste more. 'I'm so sorry.'

'Yeah. Me too.'

Mushy wasn't the way to go. He needed to be strong for them both. 'You have to forget this. Forget me. Focus on your trip.'

'That's a bit tricky when you keep kissing me.'

'I like it,' he whispered into her ear and laughed. It felt good, and sad. Sad that she made him laugh, sad that there was nowhere for them to take this. 'And you keep kissing me back. It usually takes two.'

'Well, you confuse me.'

'I confuse me too.' He tilted her chin and resisted the urge to kiss her senseless. For the first time there was honesty between them. He'd been honest. The connection tightened with understanding and mutual respect. 'I like you, Skye. A lot. But you're leaving, I'm staying. If things were different...'

Get real. Even if she were to stay, he couldn't promise her anything. Couldn't lose himself in a love that he'd most likely lose. With Skye he imagined he could love her too much. And where would that leave him? In some black hole again, only deeper and edgier than last time.

Her eyes sparkled with desire and a shot of wistfulness too. 'We keep saying it, but we keep on kissing.'

'So we should stop. Put an end to it right now. Agreed?'

'Agreed.'

'Yes, sir. Over and out.' And even as he said the words he knew it was a lie. He wanted to keep on kissing her, wanted to make up for lost time, to fill the gaping chasm that stretched beyond the next three weeks.

'Idiot!' Skye called after the motorbike rider who had overtaken them on a blind corner, breaking the silence they'd fallen into since they'd left the pub. It had been a companionable silence, though. They'd finally got their mutual appreciation out in the open. Wherever that took them. A dead end in reality, but the *'does he, doesn't he'* thing no longer applied. He did like her. And possibly wanted to take it further but for their critically stupid timing.

Old Skye would have rethought the travel, put her plans on hold and taken a chance on a future with Adam. Here in Atanga Bay.

New Skye, however, knew that doing something as foolish as hang all her dreams on a man she hardly knew would be folly indeed.

So by pulling away she'd gained a friend and some self-respect. And lost just a little hope. Count the blessings, and not the doubts.

The motorbike thundered ahead into the distance, the engine roar slowly melting into the sunny morning. She shook her head. 'This is one of the most dangerous stretches of road in the North. He's got to be doing at least a hundred and fifty.'

'Thank God you're not on a covert operation, judging enemy speed and distance. You'd have us all killed. It was about ninety.' Adam's face slipped from a smile to a frown as he steered the truck round the hairpin bends. 'But you're right, it was too fast. Kids think they're immortal.'

'You wouldn't believe the arguments Sean and I got into over his motorbike. Mum always refused to allow him to get one, so as soon as she died he went straight out and bought one.' She struggled with the crack in her voice. Her brother's betrayal bit deep. 'It felt like another nail in her coffin.'

'You have real nice brothers.'

'Yes, I do, underneath somewhere. I'm working on them. Dad wasn't such a great role model.' Unless you wanted to be a hard-nosed, deserting coward. 'The motorbike is just another hurdle.'

He scrubbed his chin with his palm. 'So now's not the time to confess about my Harley?'

'You have a motorbike?' The more she knew him, the more he shocked her. 'I guess I shouldn't be surprised.'

'Why?'

'Still waters running deep and all that... I can imagine you on a bike.' Clad in black leather, the lone brooding soldier riding off into the distance. Crikey, her imagination ran riot. She'd clearly read too many romance novels. 'What colour is it?'

'Typical woman. Not what cc, or what model? It's pink with purple stars.' He smiled again. Seemed he was letting loose a little, those smiles were coming all too frequently. 'Joke. Black and chrome.'

She loved the new ease between them, that their agenda now was only building friendship, nothing hidden. 'Of course, black and chrome, standard issue. Is there any other kind?'

'Lots. The truck's my alter ego, a cover.' He winked. 'Have you ever been on a motorbike?'

'No way. It's far too dangerous. I know the risks.'

'Not if you're sensible and take it steady. I'm not like

that madman up ahead. Definitely not with you on the back.'

'Maybe, I don't know. I've always been a teeny bit scared of them, and the power of them.' But the thought of riding on the back of his bike appealed.

'You want to live a little? A balloon ride, travel to exotic places…planes…' He shuddered. Really shuddered at the word 'planes'. Was he scared of heights? Flying? Was that how he knew the answer to the phobia question? It certainly explained the hot-air balloon freeze. Was that the demon he'd been chasing?

But he continued talking, a big smile on his lips now as he talked animatedly about something he obviously loved. 'It's nothing compared to the thrill of a bike. The wind in your face, out in the elements. It's unreal. Come on, do one more wild thing before you go. Give me a chance to show you what you're missing.'

I already know. 'Maybe, a big maybe. And don't ever tell Sean. He'll accuse me of double standards.'

'Do you care? You're a grown adult. And so is he.'

The road made a dogleg through a chicane. Bush and pasture rushed by in swift succession as the smell of eucalyptus and salt air filtered through her open window. 'But I'm still being a role model. Is your bike here in Atanga Bay? I haven't seen you on it.'

'A mate has it, with a lot of my other stuff. I've got to pick it up next week in Auckland when he's back home on leave. I have a job and a home now. Ha! He won't believe it.'

You have a mate? Well, of course he did. Why wouldn't he? Lots of mates. And a family too, no doubt. It struck her that she still didn't know much about him at all. 'Is that where you grew up? In Auckland?'

'West Auckland, Northland, wherever they could place

me.' He smiled and explained. 'Foster-care from an early age. My parents died in a car crash when I was young. I joined the army to be part of something more solid.'

That explained a lot. There was something of the loner and lost boy still deep in him. 'I see why you'd do that. To make you feel like you belonged to something bigger than yourself? Or is that my pop psychology working overtime again?'

He nodded. 'I guess.'

'We may have had our ups and downs. Lots of downs, but I love being part of a big family— Wha—?'

A plume of black smoke rose in front of them. A sense of foreboding tripped down her spine. Goose-bumps rose along her arms as her heart slammed against her ribs. 'Please, no.'

CHAPTER EIGHT

EVERYTHING froze for a second as Skye took stock of the scene in front of her. The smell of scorched tyres hit her nose. Adam's arm reached firmly across her chest. 'Stay here, Skye. I'll go take a look.'

'No. I'm coming with you. I'm not soft, I'm a nurse, for goodness' sake. I'll be a lot more use out there.' She pushed his arm away. He was protecting her, she knew, and she liked him all the more for it. Adam the protector to add to the list of soldier, lifesaver, wonderful kisser. But she didn't need protection. 'Don't mother me.'

'No, ma'am. I wouldn't dare.' He slid her a grin and made his way out of the truck straight to the motorbike rider.

The driver of the car involved in the crash staggered towards Skye as she hastily unfastened her seat belt and jumped outside. 'He just came out of nowhere. Too fast. I couldn't stop. Is he okay?'

As she closed the distance Skye assessed the car driver. No obvious bruising, cuts or grazes. Hands trembling. Ashen-faced. Shocked. She steered him to the verge. 'Sit down here. Are you hurt? Any passengers?'

'No. Just me. I'm shaky. But okay. He flew over the top of my bonnet. I just couldn't stop.'

'I know. It's okay. I understand.' She bit back a retort about the motorbike rider. This was what speed did.

Forget about cosy Harley rides for two.

She looked over to where Adam worked on the injured rider. His competence settled her. He was the perfect guy to have around in an emergency. Calm, focused and proficient. She turned back to the car driver. 'Have you got a mobile phone? Can you phone for an ambulance? Now. Tell them we're on the Old Atanga Bay Road, about three kilometres out of town towards Brynderwyn. Say it's a road traffic accident, an emergency.'

Then she approached Adam and the patient, hardly daring to look as her heart thundered. The motorbike lay in a mangled mess on top of the rider's legs. Luckily he had full protective clothing and a full-faced helmet, but she knew potential dangers lurking underneath.

Even though logic told her the injured man wasn't Sean, she still steeled herself. Quickly scanning the situation, she blew out her angst. Wrong bike, wrong leathers.

But what if someone she loved was injured when she was so far away, having fun?

The thought of a crisis happening without her to sort it filled her with dread. Would they cope?

But she couldn't mother them all her life. And she couldn't take them all with her.

Maybe just one. *Adam*. Maybe, if she asked, he'd come with her.

That thought came out of nowhere. She shook it loose from her mind. The whole point of her adventure was that it was *hers*. Not to be shared, sullied or changed to fit someone else's plans. 'So, what have we got?'

Adam relayed the information he'd garnered. 'Just managed to get him to speak. Glasgow coma scale of thirteen, denies hitting head but in shock and pain. Hey, mate, what's your name?'

'M-Martin.'

Skye crouched over the patient. 'Well done, Martin. Adam here is a paramedic and I'm a nurse. We're going to help you. Where's the pain?'

'All over.'

'Then I'll start from the top.'

Adam gave her a thumbs-up sign. 'And I'll work up, once we can get that bike moved.'

A distant siren had her head jerking upwards, distracting from her assessment. 'That was quick. But they're still a long way away.'

'The sooner the better.' Adam nodded as he and the car driver lifted the bike from Martin's legs. He stared down at Martin's twisted fibula sticking out at a strange angle. 'Now, let's have a closer look. That leg looks nasty.'

Skye finished her assessment down to Martin's waist. 'Looks like a potential fractured left clavicle, some thoracic spine soreness. So we'll need a spinal board. Analgesia. Fluids. PDQ. Hard to measure anything else without equipment. Breathing fast but he appears to have bilateral air entry, just from observation. Tachycardia. Could mean internal bleeding.'

'You're good.'

'I know.' His compliments were like a power boost. 'I had a misspent youth in A and E.'

'Oh?'

'Trauma training course.' Almost completed when she'd believed she had a bright future as an ER charge nurse in London ahead of her. And then it had ended, swiftly. Too many of her life plans had gone awry.

Within minutes they had a full assessment of their patient, which would save valuable time when the ambulance arrived. Skye listened out again for the siren, her heart singing with relief as the white vehicle appeared round the corner.

While Adam relayed information to Dan, she tried to keep their patient relaxed. Difficult with that number of injuries. She kept Martin's neck stable between her hands. 'Dan's going to bring some pain relief any minute now, Martin. Just try to relax, relax. Relax. Take some big breaths. That's it.'

She stole a glance at Adam. As he stood at ease, confidently talking to Dan, she wondered what he'd seen out in the field. Nothing seemed to faze him. What gave him that strength? And just exactly what was he hiding? Great pain, for sure. Not purely physical. There was loss there too, she guessed. Her heart went out to him, to the lost, parentless boy trying to find a home. And finally he'd found one here, a job and a place that fitted. Just as she was leaving.

Adam and Dan hurried over with a spinal board and emergency equipment. They all focused on Martin, recognising the urgency required to stabilise him. Dan tapped the back of Martin's hand. 'I've got an injection here, mate. It'll make you feel better. Then we can get you on the road. Just a little scratch.'

With those words Skye's eyes sought out Adam's again and found him staring at her. His eyes held warmth and compassion. Memories of the balloon flight and that kiss simmered around them.

No matter how hard she tried to steer away from his magnetic presence, something pulled her back. A look, a memory, his rough-hewn face that hid so much.

Would it be like this for the next few days? Would it be like this as she stepped onto the plane? Searching him out to share a private joke, missing him? Her throat filled. God knew, she'd tried everything not to get involved with him, but somehow she'd failed. Miserably. The only thing she could think of now was how little time they had left. And what on earth they could do to make the most of it.

'Rucksack, credit cards, tickets. Tick. First-aid kit…must get that sorted out. Organise farewell party.' Skye sat at her kitchen table, running through her list, planning a final shopping trip. The late March sunshine filtered through the open back door as a gentle hum of bees and next door's tractor rumbled on the shimmering airwaves.

By some miracle, she had nothing to do. Her brothers had heeded her threats and cleaned the place up. And although it wasn't perfect, they'd attempted vacuuming and swung a duster around. There was even space on the table to lay out her scrapbooks and dream awhile. A perfect summer Sunday. Alone. At peace.

Eleven days.

And then no more perfect summer Sundays here in Atanga Bay. A tightness clutched her throat, shifting the peace to the back burner. This place held so many lovely memories. And too many sad ones. Although it would hurt to leave, she needed something fresh and new in her life.

Focusing on the last-minute things to do helped take her mind off a tinge of apprehension. The ache in her chest. Adam. Their kisses. The way she'd felt when he'd held her tight. The way she'd never felt with any man before. She'd given up so much for others and now the thought of giving him up too pierced her. Giving him up so she could live her life. She laughed and hit her head with her fists. 'Oh, Adam, what have you done to me?'

Easing out her shoulders, she eased her neck from side to side. Mooning over maybes wouldn't get her to Paris. 'Okay. Concentrate, Skye Williams. Buy travel clothes, camera.' She flipped open her laptop. 'Hmm, which one should I get?'

'I always like an SLR myself.' Adam's deep voice rumbled around the kitchen blasting her serenity to pieces. 'Pricy, but better clarity, great for distance shots.'

Her heart lurched into her throat. 'Whoa! You made me jump.'

'Clearly.'

'How long have you been there?'

'Not long.' He stepped into the kitchen and grinned. Dressed head to toe in black, his leather jacket completing his bad-boy image, he looked seriously gorgeous. Skye's brain and body went into overdrive. Had he heard her mooning over him?

Embarrassing. White noise rushed through her ears as blood reached her cheeks.

If he had heard her, he didn't let on. 'Looks nice in here. Have you been busy mothering again?'

'No. *I* didn't do a thing.' Embarrassment evaporated into self-satisfaction. She pointed to the clean sink and tidy table. 'I need to thank you. Seems to be becoming a habit. One of these days I'll do something good for you too. Then we'll be even.'

'Oh?' He leaned on the back of a chair. 'What kind of good?'

Was it her imagination but did his eyes twinkle?

Mysterious Adam Miller had twinkling eyes. Who would have known?

'You've just about created a miracle in my house.'

'Ah. The note?'

'Absolutely. It worked as a great starting point. Then I was on a roll. I told them I'd throw away anything I found on the floor, and when Stevie lost his brand-new pulling shirt to the black bin-liner they started to take me seriously.' She smiled, thinking of the horror on her brother's face as he'd realised that, for once, she'd meant business. Adam had given her confidence to tackle this, given her wings, and she'd taken flight. 'There's hope for them yet.'

'Well done, you.'

'But it was your note that started it.'

'And it was you who followed through.'

Pride filled her smile. Yes. She'd followed through. Her brothers had sat up and taken note when she'd started to draw on a strength that had lain dormant too long. She glanced around the room. 'But I don't want to think about what will happen after I've gone.'

'Neither do I.' He shrugged, and his words hung in the air. She looked away, unable to think further than this minute with him. Contemplating a future without him confused her.

Somewhere along the line Adam had changed. Opened up a bit, let loose. Brightened. Shadows still lurked behind those eyes, but not as dark as when she'd first met him. She felt like she knew him at a deeper level, recognised a connection of spirit, and understood his need for privacy. God knew, she'd valued her own space when the Brian tornado had ripped through her life. And yet there was so much about Adam she wanted to learn, to explore.

He leaned closer. 'Are you busy right now?'

Not any more. 'I'm just finishing up. Thought I might go and visit Mim's baby later.'

'Well, I hope you don't mind me calling in unannounced, but I've just got back from Auckland. Brought *my* baby to show you.'

'Ba—?' The penny dropped as she reviewed his leathers. 'Oh, your bike. I thought I heard something…a tractor.'

He didn't miss a beat. 'Sacrilege! My Harley does not sound like a tractor. Come and listen.'

'I don't think so. I can't forget what happened to Martin. Three surgeries to fix his broken bones. It's too dangerous.'

His hand squeezed her shoulder. Martin had been lucky, they both knew it. They'd shared so much these past couple of weeks. A new life, an almost death. The biggies. Each experience deepened her respect for Adam. Each minute in his company revealed layers to him that she admired. Adam was solid, loyal and competent. Not dangerous.

'I'm not asking you to ride her at speed round hairpin bends. I'd never ask you to do something that freaked you, Skye. Just come outside and listen to the way she purrs. Just for a second.'

His enthusiasm was infectious. 'She? Your bike has a gender?'

'Doesn't your car?'

'No, it's a heap of metal.'

He looked horrified and amused in equal parts. 'Oh, Skye. Where's your romantic heart?'

'It did a runner a few years back.'

'So, let's go and find it again.' His hand grabbed hers and before she knew it she was in bright sunshine staring at the most amazing motorbike she'd ever seen. Clean, sleek edges, mirrored chrome and a jet black that somehow sparkled in the dappled sunshine.

Pride edged Adam's stance. His chin lifted as he flicked the keys in the ignition. A deep sonorous purr—yes, the only way to describe it—shivered through the bike.

She smiled, happy to see him so animated. 'It…sorry, *she*…' Skye winked at him '…is beautiful. You're right.'

'Twist this towards you, just a little.' He took her fingers and curved them round a handlebar thing.

She twisted. The bike roared. She jumped back, relinquishing the power. 'Whoa!'

'Music to my ears.'

She put space between her and the bike, almost bumping into Adam. 'Noisy. Dirty. Dangerous.'

'Just the way I like it,' he growled into her ear, sending shivers of lust spiralling down her spine.

Putting her hands against his chest, she stared up and searched his face. 'Hello? Who are you and what have you done with Adam? Because you are definitely not him.'

'I'm just taking a leaf out of your book. Writing a new chapter. It's about time. Here.' He slung his leather jacket over her shoulders. It smelt of man, sex, Adam. She automatically threaded her arms through the warm sleeves, imagining the feel of him twined around her. The hairs on the back of her neck peaked as she hugged herself. His smile warmed her. 'It definitely suits you, all that black. But then you know that anyway.'

'Thank you.' First time a man had ever complimented her on her clothing choice.

Adam's thick, long-sleeved black T-shirt outlined his muscles and broad shoulders. She tried not to stare. But he didn't. He just kept on gazing at her with brooding dark eyes that made her feel giddy. Maybe he'd like the way she looked naked. Maybe he wouldn't ridicule her.

She'd never get the chance to find out. 'So, we're playing dress-up?'

His eyes twinkled again. 'Later, if you want to. Right now, we're going for a ride.'

'No way. Absolutely not.' Taking a step back, she shook her head. 'I said… That accident…'

His gaze bore into her, suffused her with calm. He took her by the shoulders and pulled her to face him. 'Hey. Hey. Do you trust me?'

Whoa. Another biggie. Did she? With her life, yes. With her heart? No. Trusting any man to be honest and open and loving, after Brian, proved impossible. And yet…she could, perhaps. In a different lifetime, when the clock wasn't ticking. 'I suppose.'

'I'd never hurt you, or take a dangerous risk with you. It was my job for years to assess danger before anything else. So forget that accident, Skye. He was stupid and unlucky. I don't have a death wish.' His voice dropped to soothing, calming. He closed the distance in a single stride, stuck a helmet over her head. 'Now, do not say a word about hat hair. In fact, do not say anything at all. Stay there. Give me two minutes.'

He strode to the back garden, snatched a handful of things from the washing line and stuffed them into a pannier. 'Didn't think you'd make it so easy. You're already wearing jeans and sneakers. Perfect. And your togs were just hanging there on the line, waiting for me.'

'Togs?' What was going on?

In answer to her stare he winked. 'For later. To cool down. You'll need it, this baby is hot. Now get on.'

'Wha—?' Her fledgling courage disappeared into the ether. 'No.'

'Play it your way, then.' He wrapped an arm round her waist and lifted her feet from the ground. She screamed but he jerked her higher and left no room to wriggle. 'Don't worry, I'll be gentle.'

Her rear moulded to the leather seat, the feel of the engine ticking over pulsed beneath her. Excitement rushed through her veins. Adam. A motorbike. So much for a peaceful Sunday afternoon. Undeterred, she bashed on the broad back of the hulk now sitting in front of her. 'This is kidnapping, you know.'

His head turned so she got his profile. All angles and crags, accentuated by the helmet. 'You know anyone who can afford a ransom?'

'No.' She couldn't help a playful pout forming.

'Good. Then let's go. Hold on to me. You don't have to lean or anything, just feel the corners. Enjoy.'

Enjoy? And then some. The sheer power and roar overwhelmed her, tingles of excitement thrilled down her spine. The metal thrummed. Countryside whizzed by in a haze. Wind rushed into her face. People stopped and waved. Seemed everyone knew a fancy bike when they saw it. Or was it just seeing the hunk of a rider?

Every now and then her helmet jolted against Adam's. She adjusted her posture, leaned her face against his back. Wrapped her arms around his waist, felt his heat, the vitality that had grown since he'd come to Atanga Bay, like his confidence, his ease. And this, doing something he so obviously loved, made her feel he was giving her a glimpse into his private world. He rode with precision and skill, and not once did she feel unsafe.

All too soon they pulled off the main road into a secluded layby deep in the heart of the bush. Atanga Falls, a scenic waterfall, was a popular spot for locals away from the busy beach scene. She knew it well.

'How was that?' Adam shook his head as he removed his helmet. His hair tufted in wayward spirals and she itched to smooth it between her fingers. He helped her undo the chin strap of her helmet and his fingers against her skin unleashed a torrent of need rushing through her. 'Do you believe me now?'

'Wow. Just wow…' Oxygen finally filled her lungs. The usually muted green of the bush appeared more vivid and lush, the sound of the cicadas in the searing heat clicked more loudly than normal. And Adam…she inhaled to steady herself against the buzz of it all…just looked more damned handsome than ever.

She levered off the helmet and ruffled the perspiration out of her hair. Hat hair be damned, she'd bet she looked like a lopsided hedgehog. But she didn't care. For once. Adam accepted her the way she was, not some image of a woman he wanted her to be. He'd made that clear. 'What an absolute thrill.'

'I'll make you a petrolhead yet.' He grinned. 'So you see the attraction? You'll get off Sean's back?'

'Not until he's taken an advanced driver's course. You were safe, but he's still young and inexperienced.'

'Shh, worry-wart.' He pressed a finger to her lips then smiled. 'He's a big boy now, making adult decisions. You have to let him go, and the others too.'

'They're all I have and I feel guilty about leaving them.'

His features darkened as the sun darted behind a cloud. 'Trust me on this, guilt is a useless and pointless emotion. It achieves nothing but a lot of heartache and grey hairs. You can spend your life wishing you'd done something different but it won't change a damn thing. I know.' She wanted to ask him what he meant, but he tipped her chin to face him and smiled.

'Now, how about I dig out some information about a special motorbike course I did in Auckland? If you like, I can talk to him?'

'Would you? He could do with a decent male to give him some pointers. While you're at it, could you mention the oily rags in my kitchen, the greasy handprints—'

He shook his head and threw his gloves onto the bike seat. 'Hey, honey, some battles you've just got to fight yourself.'

'Spoilsport.' She stuck her tongue out, amazed at how far they'd come in such a short time. Not long ago he'd glared at her from jagged rocks on the beach. Now she felt like she'd known him half her life, rather than half a month.

He pointed to the Atanga Falls sign. 'Do you know this place? I asked around and heard it was a good picnic spot.'

He'd asked around. He'd made an effort for her. Why did all signs point to him being perfect when all their stars were so totally out of line? 'It's our local secret. The best place to hide from the tourists. A picnic would be lovely but I didn't pack anything to eat. Suddenly I'm famished.'

He unclipped a pannier and shook it towards her. 'I have plenty of food and togs. Lead the way. Let's cool off.'

This time of day at a weekend the waterfall was often teeming with people, but the car park was empty.

Her heart skipped a little. Fear? Excitement. Going into the wilderness with a man like Adam accompanied by her out-of-control hormones could only lead her into trouble. Way more danger than a thousand-cc Harley.

But the temptation of the cool water to salve the heat wrestled with the risk of snatching some time alone with him. She wanted to believe cool water won out, but it came a paltry second. 'Watch your step. It's a bit higgledy-piggledy.'

Although he never mentioned his limp, she'd noticed it had worsened recently. But guessed he wouldn't thank her for any concession to an injury.

'Higgledy-piggledy? What century are you from? You crack me up sometimes.' His deep, mellow laugh echoed through the bush, then he kissed the tip of her nose. Effortless. The most natural thing in the world. But the heat in his gaze set butterflies flying in her stomach.

The air filled with electric static. Reaching out to touch him would be child's play. Kissing him back would be easy.

Leaving him would be so damned difficult.

She set off at a brisk pace down the narrow path, trying to rid her body of the sudden onslaught of more heady hormones. Adam stayed close behind her, his even breathing not challenged by the steep trail.

Tall ferns swayed in the breeze, illuminated by fingers

of sunlight. Black velvet tui birds flitted from branch to branch, calling, wooing, singing to each other. The path wound down to the trickling silver riverbed, taking them deeper and deeper into territory Skye knew very well. And to a destination she could only imagine.

CHAPTER NINE

ADAM followed Skye's cute sway as they descended along a winding trail towards the secluded waterhole. In the distance a low rumble of water beckoned them closer.

Pain shivered through his ankle with every footstep. Damn. He needed to get that looked at before it rendered him totally lame. He could never find the time to make a trip to the specialist. Didn't want another round of surgeries and then told it was unfixable.

They turned a corner and Skye paused. 'Here we are. Atanga Falls.'

On three steep sides a swathe of black rock had been carved out by millennia of water flowing, creating a huge natural chasm. Down one side a cascade of white water dropped hundreds of feet into the deep midnight-blue pool in front of him. Three smaller pools stepped off from the larger one then gave way to the river.

'My turn for wow. This is such a cool place to live. I'm amazed that this is here and hardly anyone knows about it.'

He'd imagined a horde of kids, families, dogs. A cacophony of noise. Not gentle birdsong and peace. They were utterly, completely alone. Alone with Skye and her fabulous body and mind-blowing smile. Alone with the frenetic buzz that sparked every time their eyes connected.

A mixture of regret and lust collided in his gut. Self-indulgence had fuelled his desire to bring her here, to ride his motorbike, to spend a few precious moments with her. He'd tried to convince himself it had been a friendly gesture. The safety of a popular public place. To show her that she deserved to be treated like the beautiful woman she was. Not made to feel small or worthless, or whatever else her ex had made her feel.

To prove he was more of a man than Brian. That he could do friends. That he wasn't out to hurt her.

Skye took off her trainers and placed them underneath a picnic table, then folded his jacket on top. 'Have you got my swimsuit? I'm so-o-o hot.'

Yes, you are. He swallowed deeply and handed her the striped costume he'd snatched from the line. Every part of him strained for her. This was such a mistake. He couldn't do nonchalant, or friends, and the only way they were headed was towards a whole lot of hurt.

As if he could stop.

She grabbed her togs and hid behind a thick cluster of *nikau* trees and bush ferns. 'Hey. No peeking.'

'Or what?' he joked, and pretended to peer through his fingers. He hadn't a hope of seeing anything but, hell, it didn't hurt to try.

'Or I dunk you.' In no time at all she whizzed past, a blur of black and a lingering scent of vanilla, then dived deep into the large pool.

Good idea. He needed something to douse his growing ardour. In a battle between errant sex drive and icy water, sex drive rarely won. He shucked off his boots and jeans, ripped off his T and followed her in.

The cool water sucked out the air from his lungs as he plunged deep into the lagoon. Refreshing and startlingly clear, he saw the pool bed deep below but touching it was impossible. It seemed endless, visible but far out of reach. Like Skye. And anything he could have with her.

As he righted himself and hit the surface he dragged in a breath. 'Yeehah!'

'Lovely?' She floated towards him, splashing arcs of droplets into the air. Sunlight glinted off the tiny waves she'd kicked across the surface of the pool. It was perfect. Sunshine, a beautiful woman. A full heart.

And she was here, so close, hair slicked back across her head, rivulets of water running down her collarbone.

As he'd driven through the country roads with her clinging to his back his heart had swelled. Pride suffused with warmth at having her wrapped round him. She'd turned his world upside down. Shuffled him along somehow from grumpy victim to a man with purpose. He'd found pride working next to her, wanted to succeed for her. Since that last day in service he hadn't wanted to achieve anything for a long time. Too chewed up by regret. But resolve and hard work—and Skye—had made him see things differently.

An arm's length away. That's all Skye was. One arm-span. God, the temptation to touch her ate into him like acid. How could he pretend to be all things nice when he wanted her, here, now?

He kicked to the centre of the pool. 'It's spectacular.'

'Watch this.' She slid out of the water and began to climb up the sheer rock wall, finding tiny footholds and grabbing for sparse tree roots. Horror raked at Adam's gut as he watched her reach out and loosen her footing. Lunging to the side, she tugged hard on a root and straightened. 'Ta-da! Want to join me?'

No. 'Skye. Get down.'

'Why?'

'It's slippery. Come on. Down.' His heart thundered as he fought panic. Too much air between the rock and the water. Too many jagged edges to cut her to shreds. It spooked him. If she slipped... 'Crazy woman. It's dangerous.'

'Hey! Stop mothering me!' She stuck out her tongue, giggled and called down from a ledge ten feet above him. 'Count me down. Five! Four...'

'No.'

'Three-two-one.' Spreading her arms out wide, she bent her knees and dived high out towards the pool.

He held his breath as she curved into the water. Deeper and deeper, until she was lost to him. But she hadn't fallen. She'd be okay. He willed his heart to slow.

Treading water, he waited for her to surface thinking of all the things he wanted to say to her. Fool. Dangerous. Careless.

He waited.

Was it some kind of game to her? The sun hid behind a cloud, shadowing his view. The ripples melted away, leaving a flat surface.

Waited...

She should have come up by now. Even he'd be stretched to the limits.

Waited...

'Shoot, Skye.' He filled his lungs with air and dived down. Disturbed mud and shale blurred his vision. He grappled around to feel something. Anything. Came up with bits of rock.

When his lungs were fit to burst he kicked hard to the surface. Still no Skye. His heart beat a raging tattoo. Where the hell...?

'Hey. What took you so long?' She tapped him on the back of his head. He swivelled to find her treading water, head tipped back. Laughing. Alive.

Thank God.

'What on earth were you doing?'

'Trying to touch the bottom. I managed it once, when I was about fifteen.'

Adrenalin blended with frustration and a weird sense of relief. 'Is that it? I thought you'd… Don't you ever…?'

She put her finger to his lips, just like he'd done earlier. 'Hey, don't be so serious. It was just a joke.'

'Skye, in my line of work stuff happens. It's messy and ugly.'

'Mine too. Which is why I like to have fun in my down time.' She grinned her winning smile and her eyebrows rose. Jabbing him in the stomach with her finger, she laughed. 'You want to have fun, don't you?'

She didn't need to tell him he'd played the overprotective card. He couldn't help it, he'd been trained to protect, to kill for those he loved. His country, his fellow soldiers.

But her cheeky smile was infectious and he allowed the corners of his mouth to match hers.

Ah, to hell with it. He didn't want to shout at her. He burned to feel her in his arms. Hold her tight. Never let her go. 'Come here, you wretched woman.'

'Why, soldier boy? What do you want?' Her voice cracked with a deep huskiness that tugged at his groin.

'I want you.' He was too far gone for lies or pretence. Drunk on the worry of losing her, the sheer pleasure of being with her. Pulling her close, he cupped the back of her neck and planted his lips on hers. Drops of water sparkled along her lashes like jewels as her eyelids fluttered shut. When she opened them again he saw surprise there. Surprise and a heat that connected somewhere deep in his soul.

Kissing him with her eyes open deepened that connection. Blatant heat, blatant want, blatant need.

'Am I dreaming?' She wriggled against him, pressed her mouth against his.

'No, this is real. Every bit of it.'

'Good.'

Her tongue licked against his, sending lust arcing through him. His need to be inside her was obvious and ardent. So much for cold water.

But they couldn't do anything here. He had no protection. Could never allow himself to take a risk of that magnitude.

He pulled away. 'Skye. I don't think…'

'No.' She pressed her mouth against his again, hunger and desire radiating from her. 'Don't think. Thinking is bad. Just feel. Dream.'

Clamping her legs around his waist, she hoisted herself above him, her breasts pressing against his shoulder. His palms fitted snugly under her bottom and he held her there, feeling the weight of her, neat and perfect in his arms.

Slowly she nibbled against the corner of his mouth, then traced a trail across his cheek.

As she neared his scar he couldn't stop the involuntary stiffening of his muscles.

'Hey. Relax.' She ran her thumb against it, felt the edges. 'Does it hurt?'

'No.' *Just the memory.*

'Poor you. I bet you were so brave.' She fitted her mouth over his, tasting, plundering, taking him close to the edge.

No. This was brave. Allowing his heart to flutter around her, allowing her close. His hands smoothed over her skin, ran up her back to the ties of her swimsuit. He slipped the knot and let her breasts fall free, her beaded nipples brushing against his chest. He palmed one, rubbing the pink bud, which brought a deep guttural moan from her throat.

Through the lust-filled smog in his brain he almost

forgot to tread water, plunging them deeper underwater, but he caught her, lifted her to the pool edge and laid her on a blanket.

Skye nuzzled against his bare chest. Her whole body sang with need and arousal. She ran shaking fingers through the smattering of dark hair that made him more masculine, more real.

Thank God the lack of condom had made them stop. Because nothing else would have. Certainly not common sense. 'Well, that broke the ice.'

Broke the ice and muddied everything.

'Shattered it, I'd say.' Adam ran his hands through her hair and massaged her head. She'd never seen him so passionate and so confident. His kisses had been wild yet soft. But where the hell they went from here, she couldn't fathom. They both had enough issues to keep them apart, different futures. She just knew she didn't want it to end.

But it had to.

His heart thumped solidly and regularly, steady beneath her cheek. 'Are you hungry?'

'Starving.'

He lifted her off him as if she were a featherweight, the definition of his biceps hardly taxed by her too-many kilograms.

'Then let's eat.' He set the pannier between them in the middle of the blanket and brought out a plethora of tubs.

Her mouth watered, but she made a mental check of the calorific content of every mouthful. Always way too many. 'Look at all this food. I'll have to double my runs or I'll never fit into my clothes.'

'Skye, give it up. You are perfect just the way you are.' His hand cupped her cheek as he tilted his head to the side and surveyed her. 'What did he do to you?'

'Brian?' Just saying the name filled her with anger.

She'd been a sap and a mug and desperate for affection. She'd believed she'd loved him. She'd been out of her mind. 'Why spoil a perfect day, talking about him?'

'Because it might help. Because he damaged you, made you believe you're one thing when you're the exact opposite. You're generous and kind. Loving, free spirited and beautiful. And he wasn't worth the dirt on your shoe.' He picked up a stone and weighed it in his hand. 'If only I had a gun.'

She couldn't help the surprised chuckle. 'What? That's a bit extreme. He only said I was fat.' *And ugly, and worthless. Unlovable.* Cementing her long-held beliefs into reality. Like her mother before her, she'd allowed the man she'd loved to take hold of her insecurities and pound them into her psyche. *Unlovable. Not good enough.*

Why the hell she'd stayed with him so long she didn't know now. Back then she'd believed she couldn't do any better.

'No!' Adam joined in the laughter. 'Hell, no. Not what you're thinking. I wouldn't waste a bullet on him. In the army, when we were really angry about something—and eight months' deployment away from family often threw up a lot of anger—at target practice we used to fire off rounds and say things to exorcise them. Here...' He gave her a rock. 'Give this a go. Throw it in the water, with all your strength. Hard, now.'

'Wumph.' She chucked it in. It dropped pathetically a few feet away.

'Is that all you can do? Try harder. Watch.' He wrapped his fist around another stone. 'Say this...*damn your lies.*'

He drew his arm back and curved the stone hard and fast into the centre of the pool.

Grabbing a similar-sized stone, she copied him. 'Damn your lies.'

'That was so lame. Were you angry with him, or just a little bit peeved?' He stood behind her, lifted her arm and pulled it back, wrapping his other arm around her stomach. His voice instilled determination in her. His breath, so close to her neck, sent a sigh shuddering through her. With him close anything seemed possible and the rubbish Brian had fed her couldn't touch her again. 'Say it louder, and lob the stone deep into the water.'

'Damn your lies.' She threw the stone and watched it disappear with a satisfying splash. Heat burned her cheeks. 'I feel stupid.'

'No, you don't. Now. What else?'

'Damn your broken promises.' She picked up another stone, threw it further, wondering what words Adam had shouted at the firing range. What pain he'd endured, not just physical pain, she was sure of it. 'What would you say?'

'This isn't about me. This is just about you.' His face creased into a smile. 'That's it. Again.'

'Damn your jibes about my body.' Whoosh. He was right. Letting go felt good. Better than good. Powerful, strong. Able to conquer anything. The inner strength she'd lost for so long came rushing back. 'Damn your sordid tutor room.'

Whoosh. Splash.

Adam frowned, paused with his arm in mid-air. 'Tutor room?'

'Shh. I'm on a roll. Damn your—'

'Tutor room?' He reached behind her and gripped the stone.

'Yes. He was my tutor.' Blood rushed to her face as the unfettered truth flew out. 'Yes. It couldn't get any more seedy. He was my tutor and married. I had no idea I was committing the greatest sin in my book. And I gave up everything for him, my future, dreams, plans, just because he asked. Stupid fool.' The stone slipped from her grip. 'I guess it made no difference in the end. I had to come back here for Mum anyway.'

'But you could have had years before that, enjoying your dream.' He grabbed for the stone, pulled his arm back with full force, concentration and anger warring in his eyes. 'Damn your tutor room. Damn you.'

Then he sent the stone spiralling into the air, hitting the far side of the waterfall with a thump.

His hands fisted by his sides as he gulped in air.

When he'd wrestled his breathing back to normal, he took her hand. 'Not all men are like him. He misused his position, took advantage of you. You were taken for a ride, Skye. A long one.'

'And I don't want to talk about him ever again.' Adam was different. A real man, caring, tender. She could love him, perhaps. Given time. Her arms ached with the effort of throwing the rocks but a strange, deep calm wrapped itself around her. Brian's taunts had been exorcised from her brain. She wouldn't let anyone treat her like that again. She deserved better. She deserved the best. 'I feel so much better.'

'Don't ever let anyone treat you like that again, do you hear me? Don't give anything else up—go out and do what you want to do.'

If she knew what that was now. 'Yes, sir.'

The shadows that had flitted across his eyes disappeared and he led her back to the picnic. 'Now you are going to eat. A decent amount.'

Her stomach growled. At the back of her mind the niggling fat mantra ticked, but for the first time in a long time she chose to ignore it. 'Yes. Watch out, there'll be none left for you.'

'I don't care. Just seeing you relaxed and enjoying yourself is good enough for me. Now, there's German salami, French Brie, Italian ciabatta, Greek olives and tzatziki.'

'Ooh, what a feast. Yum.'

'You got it. A European feast.' His bright face told her he'd put more than a little thought into this. 'And best of all, your favourite, champagne. French, obviously.'

'Ah…because I'm going to Europe? You didn't have to do all this. For me.'

'Yes, I did.'

Instead of the elation she expected, a profound sadness weighed on her chest. He'd gone to a huge effort. It was such a simple thing, bringing her for a picnic, showing her his bike, sharing his life. But no one—*no one*—had ever made her feel this special.

'I didn't know exactly where you were going, so I took a punt.' He offered her the bread and flipped the lid open on the dip.

Scooping some yoghurty cucumber onto the ciabatta, she ate, tucked into some olives and salami, then spoke. The pleasure of talking about the trip she'd planned from childhood was tinged with the thought of leaving. 'I start out in Asia, actually. A quick fifteen-day tour of Cambodia, Laos and Vietnam.'

'Darn it, I should have brought spring rolls, I knew it.' He popped the champagne and filled two plastic flutes. 'Here, enjoy. To your trip.'

'Thanks. To my trip.' Which was fast becoming a confusion of liberation, nerves and regret. The bubbles made her nose twitch as she took a sip. Would her trip be as exciting as sitting here in a familiar place with a man she'd grown very fond of? Too fond of. Somewhere along the line his strength and steadiness had snagged her heart. She fought back a lump in her throat. 'Then I fly to Athens. Ten days island hopping, the usual Kiwi pilgrimage over to Gallipoli, then I scoot to Italy. I'm going to take the train south to north, stopping off at the usual places— Rome, Sienna, Florence, Milan—then meander through France, Belgium…'

'Not Spain?'

'I'd love to visit Spain and Portugal, but I haven't got time. I start my new job at St Barts at the end of June.'

His eyes widened. 'You have a job too? Not just a short trip, then home?'

'I wouldn't dare go without a definite job offer. I couldn't afford to flit about and travel for years. I'm finally going to work in A and E properly. In London, the centre of everything.'

'Good for you. You'll have a ball.' He shifted away a little. Leaned up against a tree, crossed his ankles and took a long drink.

She edged closer, suffering the cold now he'd moved. She pressed her palm against his dragonfly tattoo. Just so she could feel him, vibrant under her fingers. Taking courage in both hands, she told him what she'd been thinking for the last few days. 'I'll miss you.'

He wrapped his arm around her shoulders and hugged her, more like a brother would do than a lover. Pressed a chaste kiss on her head then inched away.

That was it, then. He was shutting down. The talk of her leaving had knocked sense into him after all. 'No, you won't miss me, or Atanga Bay. You'll be too busy having a great time. A new life. Just like me, here.'

The rash words *Come with me* came into her mouth. But she couldn't say them. Couldn't ask him to give this up. His new life. She knew too well that giving things up only caused resentment in the end. Knew it because she'd lived it.

Tears burnt her eyes. Focusing on something else, anything, she ran her index fingertip over the black and yellow insect hovering over his heart. 'Tell me about this.'

His back stiffened minutely, but enough to speak volumes. 'Another time, maybe.'

'Don't you dare close down on me now, Adam Miller.' She folded her arms across her chest. 'We've shared too much for you to go scuttling back into your shell. I've told you all my sad and sorry mistakes. I've opened my heart to you. It's only fair you do the same.'

'It doesn't work like that.' He started to gather up the picnic debris. 'I think we should go.'

'Just like that?'

'Yes. Just like that. It's getting late. And you wanted to go to Mim's you said.'

'It'll wait until tomorrow.'

His frown deepened. 'Don't ever put anything off on my account.'

'God save me from yet another stubborn, stubborn man.' She stood, dragged her T-shirt over her swimming costume. 'Just when I think we're getting somewhere, you clam up.'

'We can't get anywhere. You know that full well.' He shook his head, took a step forward and winced, favouring his left leg more profoundly as he walked along the path.

And now his foot was damned well hurting him too. But would he ever admit that? No. 'Stop, Adam. Let me take a look at your foot.'

'No. I can manage.'

He strode ahead but she caught him up, darted in front of him and thrust her hands on her hips. 'You're limping. Sit.'

He opened and closed his mouth, shrugged and sat on a rock. 'Stop fussing. It's fine.'

She dragged up his trouser leg and inspected his foot. Frustration and anger boiled through her.

'It isn't fine. It's a mess.' The skin puckered under her fingertips. A jagged ridge hit her fingers, moved slightly. It was red and bruised. He must have been in agony. 'You've got to get it seen by a doctor.'

'It's an old injury. Now stop staring at it and let's go.' He pushed the denim fabric back down and stood. 'I said it's fine. Leave it.'

'Not until you promise to get it looked at. It's only going to get worse, then you won't be able to work, or walk…'

'Hell, you turn nagging into an art form.' His mouth formed a thin line and his words stung. But she didn't care how angry he'd got. She'd match him fury for fury right now. How the hell he evoked such strong emotions in her she didn't know. One minute it was lust with a capital L. Now it was rage all rolled up in deep tenderness, knowing how much pain he must be in. How much effort he'd gone to for her. But he still wouldn't share the one thing she wanted. Himself.

'And you're the most infuriatingly stubborn man I've ever met. Promise me, right now, you'll get it seen to.'

He opened his palms to her in a conciliatory gesture. 'Okay. Okay. I'll go, soon as.' He turned and stomped ahead, his body obviously trying to compensate for his damaged leg.

Frustration clawed through her stomach. Whenever she thought she was getting somewhere, he slammed up the barriers. 'One last thing.'

He turned. 'Now what?'

Emotion after emotion rolled through her. She wouldn't

let him go without getting things crystal clear between them. 'What about this afternoon?'

He shook his head again. Didn't need to say the words written in his eyes. 'That was a mistake and we both know it.'

CHAPTER TEN

COLD night air whipped into Adam's face as he opened the throttle and let rip. Kilometre after kilometre sped by, taking him through black countryside lit by a sliver of moon.

Damn.

Nothing seemed to temper his dark mood.

He didn't know why anger ripped through him. Who he was angry at. Skye for blasting his heart wide open. Or himself for letting her. But in the end he settled on himself. Getting involved with someone else he'd lose.

He couldn't get the image of her face, as he'd dropped her off earlier, out of his head. Her eyes as black as the sky above him, her chin set and mouth clamped shut.

He'd messed up. Big time.

But whatever the future held, he at least owed her some respect, truth. A decent conversation where he didn't clam up at the slightest personal question. She'd be gone soon enough and he couldn't live with himself thinking she'd get on that plane without setting things straight between them.

Whatever straight was.

He rode for a few more kilometres, planning how, what and when. Lost in the details and the memory of her face. But when he looked up he'd stopped outside her house.

Now or never.

He banged on the door. 'Skye. Open up.'

Silence. Apart from the blood rushing through his ears. The hammering of his heart.

A light flickered on above the porch. A bleary head popped out the open window. Sean. 'Oi, mate. It's after midnight. What d'you want?'

'Skye.'

'She said not to let you in.'

'Give me a break here, man.'

'She's been a nightmare all evening.' Sean scraped a hand through matted hair. 'Aw, perhaps you can sort her out. She's in the sleep-out. Oh, and epic bike, by the way.' He threw down a key.

Adam caught it and heaved out a breath. Thank God she had brothers who broke all the rules.

He found her in the lean-to sleep-out, sitting at her desk, looking over a pile of tour brochures and her beloved scrapbooks. Even from this distance, faced with her ramrod-straight back, he knew she was hurting.

He didn't wait to be invited in. 'Skye?'

Head down, she kept her eyes on the books. 'Thought I heard your tractor. Did Sean let you in? Typical. One day he'll do what I ask.'

'He threw me a key.' He covered the distance to the desk. Thought about whipping her into his arms. Thought better of it.

The aroma of some kind of relaxing incense hit him. He took in his surroundings. Instead of the dark decor he'd expected, the room was a kind of cream colour. Not girly, but soft, feminine. Very feminine. They'd missed out on those steps—the courting, the gradual getting to know each other, the little things that allowed you to get used to someone. But they'd covered a lot of the major stuff—sharing a new life, an almost tragedy and perfect kissing. That mad quiz seemed like aeons ago, not just a matter of days.

And now he was here in her very intimate space. He didn't know where to start. He realised he hadn't really prepared anything at all. 'Am I disturbing you?'

'What? Right this second? Or just all the time, in my head?' Slamming the scrapbook closed, she turned to face him, weariness in her eyes. No brief smile. He'd never seen her looking so down. It ate him away that he'd made her feel like this. 'I'm so confused, Adam. I don't even want to think about going away any more.'

'Don't be crazy.'

'That's rich, coming from a man who shouts things while throwing stones into rivers.'

A smile uncurled from his heart, reached his mouth. 'I thought it would help.'

He watched her fight the smile playing over her lips too. She lost. 'It did. Now, what can I do for you? As you can see, I'm up to my eyes. It's also very late.'

'I came to talk.'

'Hallelujah.' A sigh shivered through her. Her eyes squeezed shut as she ran her fingers through the soft black spikes in her hair. She'd showered and changed since the waterfall, wore black PJs in a soft cotton lace combo. The top had thin straps looping over her shoulders and a deep V, revealing enough cleavage to draw his attention. The pants came mid-way down her thighs. He tried not to look. Failed. He'd already seen her almost naked at the waterfall, but the lace fired his senses. Raw need stirred in his gut, and he knew it would take more than a few kilometres on his bike to get it out of his system.

'Stop looking at me like that. You said it was all a mistake.'

'It is…was.'

She ran her fingers over a thin silver chain round her neck. 'But you want to talk.'

'I wouldn't say I want to. But I'm going to.'

'Good. I don't have any rocks to throw, so please be gentle with my stuff.' She flicked a hand. 'You'd better sit down.'

Piles of books littered the only spare chair. Clumps of clothes, travel guides, foreign currency dotted the floor. There was nowhere to sit but her bed. He shrugged off his boots and sat against the stack of surprisingly pink pillows. 'For someone who's flying out in a couple of weeks, you've got a lot of sorting to do.'

'I'm leaving most of it behind.' Wheeling the office chair to the bed, she sat, put her elbows on the duvet and rested her chin on her fists. The smile hit her eyes and blazed. 'Now quit stalling, soldier boy. I'm all ears.'

'Wow, great bedside manner. You learnt this from Freud? Jung? Dr Phil?' *Brian? The esteemed emergency medicine tutor?* The mere thought of her with another man ran like poison through his veins. But, hell, who was he to say who she could go out with? Sleep with? Love?

Love. Love? Love Skye? The thought punched him in the gut. Sent his brain reeling. It had been two short weeks. A handful of encounters. He couldn't love her.

No. He couldn't.

No. He put that decision neatly into its box and stashed it deep inside his core. No. He wouldn't love her. He wouldn't love anyone again. Not just to lose them and splinter his heart.

But he still owed her an explanation.

She chewed her bottom lip. 'I learnt a lot from raising boys. Ask a direct question, you get a grunt. Ask an indirect question, you get a grunt. Either way, it's a grunt. I might as well save myself the time and go straight for the jugular.' Placing her palm against his neck, she looked into his eyes. Everything he saw there said, *Trust me. Tell me*. And he wanted to. God knew, he wanted to. But the thought of opening his heart to her and then losing her paralysed him with fear.

She ran a finger up to his scar. 'You can start with this.'

He gripped her wrist. 'I thought you were nice.'

'Oh, I can do nice. I'll do nice when you're finished.'

Was she playing? After everything he'd put her through, the indecision, the holding back. He didn't deserve nice, he deserved open hostility. 'What kind of nice?'

'I'm great at stress relief. I do a mean foot rub. I studied aromatherapy when Mum was sick, it helped calm her down. I have oil.' The thought of her hands on his body almost had him spilling his story right there. But she held up her hand. 'Seriously, it's enough that you're here. If you don't want to tell me…'

'Hey, a foot rub? How can I resist?' His gaze settled on her hands, imagined what they could do with a drop of oil. Imagined what a night with her would be like. Or a lifetime. Filled with long kisses and sunshine.

Okay. Playtime over. He dropped her wrist and swallowed hard. He needed to have the honesty he'd promised himself. And he knew he could trust Skye, more than anyone, to understand. Trusted she wouldn't throw his hurt back in his face, or use it as a weapon to injure him further. Like he'd done too many times to himself.

But he struggled to find the right words. His shoulders shot up, his hands involuntarily curled into fists. He shut his eyes. Remembered the smoke, the shooting. Panic like static in the air, almost tangible.

He steadied his breathing. 'We were on a peace-keeping mission in Timor-Leste. Training the local army. One night we were giving chopper support to the ground patrol, ended up wandering into some kind of gangland warfare. Two gangs, one scrap of territory. God knows where they got their sophisticated weapons from, but this wasn't your average neighbourly dispute. A storm hit, and our comms went down. There was no back-up, just a weird sense of surreality and a whole lot of ferocious gunfire. These guys didn't have an argument with us, but we were stuck slam in the middle of their war.'

Her pupils widened, jet black but sincere. She knotted her fingers into the corner of the duvet. 'Scary?'

'No more than usual. We're trained to deal with any situation.' But in a blackened sky thick with lightning when everyone was the enemy, it had soon spun out of control. He dismissed the panic rising in his gut. 'We were coming in to land and the chopper took a hit. Then the pilot, Henare, got a bullet. Suddenly we were at the centre of hell, spiralling through the sky towards concrete.'

'Scary then?'

'There's hardly enough time to be scared, but a lot of space to think, *I'm going to die*. Right here in a country that doesn't want us.' The ache in his chest spread to his gut, his leg, his head. 'I didn't want to die, so I kept the image of my wife's face at the forefront of my mind as we dropped through hundreds of feet of nothing. I willed my life for her, for our marriage. For the children we'd promised to have.'

'But you didn't die. Thank God.'

'There were plenty of days I wished I had.' He shook his head, his throat almost closing with the memory. For a long time he'd been surrounded by blackness, dark moods and pain. Coming back from the edge had been a struggle. He'd done it. Just. But had lost his marriage in the process.

Now Skye's hand covered his. Warmth emanated from her touch into his cold skin. 'Post-traumatic stress can do that to you.'

'It was all kinds of crazy. My whole world fell apart and

I couldn't...' He blew out a breath. Blew out the visceral pain of losing everyone he'd ever loved. Fading now, in reality. Maybe time had finally started to heal.

'I didn't know how to talk about it. Monica tried to understand but it was too raw for me. No one tells you about that, how you have no words to express how you feel, just a deep swell of hurt and constant darkness. I didn't want to dwell on it but, no matter how much I fought it, it was there in my head the whole time. Going round and round. The psychological pain was worse than the physical. They called me a hero, but my friends were much more deserving than me. I couldn't see past that.

'Why did I live and they die? That question was all-consuming, didn't make any sense. In the end Monica and I drifted apart, lost our way.' Communication had reduced to pitying looks and guilt-ridden rants until neither of them could stand the pressure any more.

'I'm sorry.'

'Me too. It's okay.' And it was. Back then pain from the end of his marriage had meshed with his physical hurt and guilt. Melded into a fog. A fog that had begun to clear. 'She's married to someone else now. I'm happy for her. She deserves a nice guy.'

It had been a no-fault divorce, relief on both sides when the papers had come through.

Skye nodded. 'That's good. It can't have been easy for you.'

'None of it was easy.'

'But what about the rest—what you saw, what happened to you in the field—how do you let go of that?'

'I don't know if you ever do, but somehow you have to learn to live with it or you'd go mad. There was a lot of anger for a long time. I felt stripped down to my core, believing that being alive was somehow a betrayal. I lost everything I'd worked towards and watched five of my team die. I tried to save them, but it wasn't enough.'

He paused, allowing the familiar surge of regret to wash through him. If only there hadn't been a storm. If only they'd seen the trouble ahead. If only he'd died instead of Charlie O'Hara, father of four, there'd be one less family without a dad.

So many if-onlys. And none of them could change a damned thing. 'I'm a medic, for God's sake. Do no harm? Save them all? I couldn't do anything except watch the lights go out. For a long time I believed I'd let them all down.'

'No, you didn't. You mustn't believe that.'

'Survivor's guilt. I know the psychobabble. We'd been a tight team, a real force, shared so much. To while away the long hours of deployment we'd talk about our futures, dreams, plans. And then it was all blown away into dust.' He tapped his tattoo with his fist. Caught her looking at him, eyes raised in question. 'Laugh if you like, but the team and I all got the same tattoo a few days before that last deployment. A sort of Kiwi *Band of Brothers* thing.'

'Why would I laugh?'

'Some might.'

'You were part of something, had strong ties. Not many people can say they've had such loyal relationships.' She crawled next to him and laid her head against his chest. Flattened her palm over his heart. 'But why a dragonfly?'

His throat caught as he remembered their promises and the hope of those last few days before…the end. 'It symbolises a life of no regrets. Living in the moment.'

'Is that what you do?'

He laughed. Not even remotely. 'It's what I told myself I'd been doing for the last few years. I had no life plan any more, no job, no wife, few friends, and fewer who'd put up with my moods. Flitting from job to job, town to town, keeping everyone at arm's length. Doing exactly what I wanted to do and hang everyone else. Sick of the pity and the fake hero badge they all stuck on me.

'Then one day I got to thinking, no regrets means looking back and being proud of what you've done. I couldn't find a lot to be proud of right then, so I straightened myself out and got this job. I owe it to my team to have a life worth living. A decent job, doing something good, saving lives.'

He shuffled an arm around her. His mood brightened a little just because he could hold her close, the ghosts that haunted him banished back to their box. His chest felt light for the first time in years. Maybe shooting at things or throwing rocks wasn't the only way to vent. Maybe just plain old talking in the arms of a good woman could work miracles too.

'Living in the moment. I like that.' Skye lifted her head from his heart and looked into his eyes. Honesty glittered there, the shadows almost gone. If there was more to his story, she had no doubt he would tell her. Another time.

She couldn't imagine the pain he'd endured as an orphan. Then later as a medic, whose job it was to save lives, not watch his buddies die. Couldn't imagine the fear at falling through the sky, facing almost certain death.

But she knew enough about loss and hurt, how it coated every thought, every chance of happiness. She had no idea what it would be like to lose everyone she'd ever loved— losing her mother had been hard enough. To the point where the idea of getting close to someone else was scary. If you didn't love, you didn't get hurt. Small wonder Adam had closed down at the chance of intimacy.

She found him a smile. 'Thank you for being so honest with me. I'll treasure the fact that you told me.'

He laughed. 'I don't recall having much of a choice.

I didn't want you to think my reluctance to get involved had anything to do with you. But now I really should go. It's late.'

His fingers cupped her cheek. She rocked her face against his hand, closed her eyes, snatching the last moments of this day with him.

The anger she'd had as he'd closed down at the waterfall had dissipated the moment he'd walked through the door. He respected her enough to want to make amends.

And she couldn't deny the anger had been all wrapped up in wanting him. The confusion of needing him so much in her life and the knowledge she would soon be gone.

But right now, in *this moment*, with him in her bedroom, everything became clear. Honourable Adam would leave in a minute, unfettered by his demons and happy that their relationship was back on even ground. Honourable Adam would not do to her what she wanted him to do to her. Right now.

'Stay a while?' She reached over to the drawer in her bedside cabinet and took out her essential oils. The heady scent of sandalwood hit her senses first. Perfect, with a few drops of bergamot and ylang-ylang. She mixed them in a dish with carrier oil, and inhaled. The combination of woody and floral tones spiced with the citrusy bergamot kindled the fire burning inside her. Knowing she was making an aphrodisiac mix spurred her on. Her own guilty secret. 'Now for my side of the bargain.'

'Skye, you don't have to. You serious?'

'Absolutely.'

He held her gaze, direct and intense. Any caution had been replaced with a hunger she knew was mirrored in every cell in her body. She couldn't drag her eyes away from his face, the scar that had caused so much turmoil.

His agreement was silent but tacit. A quiver of excitement ran down her back. A slow ache unfurled deep inside, turning her legs to liquid.

'This works better if you lie down.' She found her voice, which had turned hoarse with desire. Stripped off his socks, placed his feet over a towel and slicked the oil onto her hands. Taking his right foot into her hand, she began to massage. His head tipped back and the tiny trace of shadows and creases left on his face melted into a picture of peace.

His leg twitched. 'Hey.'

'Tickling?'

'Yes.' His eyes shone clear blue as his mouth hitched into a smile. Free and relaxed and filled—for the first time—with a mischievous glint. 'You are the devil in disguise.'

'Perhaps. I quite like that idea.' Sex with Brian had been predictable, instigated by him, led by him and finished all too quickly. She wanted to savour this night with Adam, to enjoy the sheer delight of having him there. God knew when it would ever happen again. If she was going to live in this moment then, hell, she wanted it to last a very long time.

She tiptoed her fingers up the inside of his jeans. 'If you don't want oil on them, these will have to come off.'

Straddling his legs, she reached down and unzipped the waistband of his jeans, saw the effect her movements had had on him, the straining of his erection against the dark denim. That she had brought him pleasure with just the touch of her fingers made her feel dizzy with desire.

Angling her mouth over his, she kissed him full on, hard and fast. His tongue slid into her mouth and she tasted him, hot and male and everything she'd ever needed. His hands curved under her buttocks, the thin fabric frustratingly there, a barrier between skin on skin.

She pulled away, controlled her breathing as best she could. 'I promised you a foot rub. Don't get ahead of yourself.'

'But I want to touch you. More kissing, please.'

'Later.'

'Soon later.' He shucked down his jeans and threw them to the floor.

'Now for the other side.' Then she pushed him back onto the bed. The feeling of power made her feel light-headed. In answer to his frown she smiled. 'I'll be very careful.'

She picked up his left foot, massaged long flowing strokes along the sole.

'Okay. That's enough of that.' He flipped her onto her back and pressed against her. 'I can think of better things we could be doing.'

'Oh. Good idea,' she said mischievously. Emboldened by his directness, she put her hand to his groin, brushed across the length of him, felt the heat and his need for her. A wicked tingle coursed through her as anticipation built to fever pitch. She wanted him, now. Deep inside her, stretching and filling her. His hands touching every part of her. Stroking, caressing, kissing.

She almost melted in lust as he nuzzled her neck, nibbled along her collarbone.

He eased off her PJ top, swirled kisses around her nipples, leaving her aching for more. But he moved away to pepper feather-light kisses along her ribs. *No.*

Yes. God, he inflamed her skin each time his mouth made contact.

While her hand was on his chest she took the liberty of removing his T-shirt. Her lips were drawn automatically to the black and yellow dragonfly. She licked along the wingspan, sucked on his nipple, squirmed at the deep growl in his throat.

His tongue licked along the side of her neck as he pressed his body against her. Then he clamped his mouth on hers, infusing every cell of her body with a raging fire. Words fell away into a sublime pool of ecstasy.

Adam cradled her face in his hands as he slowed his kisses. Not easy. 'Steady. I want to take it slow.'

'Spoilsport.' Her hands ran around the top of his boxers, the light, fluttery strokes driving him to the edge. He grabbed her hand and held it against his chest. 'No. I mean it. I want to savour you.'

He wanted to give her pleasure. Not just take it for himself. To discover every part of her body, to assuage the rage of need he had for her. She'd listened to his story, understood his reluctance to share his hurt, and he'd seen genuine sorrow in her eyes. Not pity. With Skye he was a whole man, not damaged, and he wanted to show her how a real man treated a woman.

He stuck his fingers in the aromatherapy oil, rubbed his palms together and inhaled the funny smell. 'Gee, you have some kinky ideas.'

She wrinkled her nose and sniffed. 'Massage is not...'

'Shh.' His mouth stopped her flow of words. This time he imbued his kiss with every ounce of feeling he had for her. Soft and careful, he explored her, relishing her taste, the feel of her tongue against his. The bottom of her lip, the edge of her teeth, getting to know her, inch by inch, committing every part of her mouth to memory. When he'd finished with her lips he moved to her cheek, her neck, behind her ear. Nuzzling against her soft hot skin, inhaling the smell of vanilla tangled with blatant desire.

When she pulled away her lips were swollen, her eyes misted, and he ached to be inside her, to be there for ever in her arms. In her bed. Lost in her kisses.

Holding her arms above her head with one hand, he

stroked his other across her neck, down to her soft, full breast and over her nipple. The bud hardened at his touch and he sucked it into his mouth.

A low moan of pleasure urged him to repeat the action on the other breast. Her hips rocked in a slow rhythm, her eyes fluttered closed as her breathing quickened. Her fingers snagged in his hair, her legs rubbed against his in a frenzy of yearning.

As much as his body throbbed with intent he forced himself to slow down. She deserved respect, the full treatment. 'Open your eyes.'

Wide, dark eyes stared up at him as his palms smoothed across the curve of her belly. Stepping lower, lower to the inside of her thighs. He watched her pupils soften with desire, saw the question, gave her his answer. 'I want you.'

'Yes, Adam. I want you too. Now.' She wriggled her arms free and rocked against him, pressing hard, hot kisses on his lips. Then she took his erection in her hand and nearly blew his mind. Laughing, she looked up at him with *faux*-innocent eyes. 'I command you, Captain Miller. Make love to me now. Or you'll be in solitary confinement.'

'Yes, ma'am.' He licked her neck. 'Er…solitary's for prisons. Not the army.'

'Whatever.' She squeezed him gently. 'I think you know what I mean.'

Trust Skye to make this fun. Fun and sexy.

And she was leaving.

A fierce surge of pent-up emotion ripped through him. All kinds of confusion.

He couldn't think of a life without her. But he had to let her go. And be damned happy for her too. She had to live her life. What he'd be left with he didn't know. But he wanted to be with her now. That much he knew. Whatever tomorrow or next week or next year might bring.

Suddenly his desire to take it slowly got lost in over-whelming hunger.

'Condoms...' He grabbed for his wallet, ripped open a packet.

He quickly sheathed himself and laid her back down onto the bed. Found her mouth with his. Parted her thighs. She clawed at his back. 'Please, now.'

And then he was pushing into her, shifting her bottom to allow him to go deeper, harder, fuller.

Her arms wrapped around him as she pulled him close, pressing every inch of her divine body against him, her mouth on his shoulder, her teeth in his skin.

Her grip tightened around his neck as she rose in perfect rhythm with him. Her breathing became staccato and urgent. 'I didn't know it could be like this.'

'No. Neither did I.' He moved his head, clamped his gaze on hers and felt that absolute connection, the fire between them, the meeting of souls. Never in his life had his heart been so full of hope, so utterly joined with another.

As he thrust deeper he felt the delicious tightening of her muscles around him. Saw the pressure building, the moment as her eyes sparked. And joined her in the ultimate release.

CHAPTER ELEVEN

*On early shift. Didn't want to wake you. Will catch
you later. A x*

SKYE picked up Adam's scrawled note from her bedside
table and held it to her chest. *Soppy fool.* What grown-up
woman did that kind of thing? She wasn't exactly a smit-
ten teenager, she was a woman with plans for independent
travel, a new career overseas.

But she stole another look at the note.

Will catch you later.

It was a start. It was hardly *I can't live without you.* But
at least it didn't say *I made a mistake.*

Because she knew she hadn't and hoped he felt the
same. Whatever that was. Actually she hoped he felt as
wonderfully elated and satiated by their night of lovemaking, but not as muddled as she did right now. She didn't
trust her shaky emotions, hoped he had something more
stable they could cling to.

A sharp sting of tears pricked the backs of her eyes. She
had fundamentally changed. Adam had changed her. Not
just the sex, which had been immensely brilliant, but his
gentle, tender touch, his belief in her, the intense passion

in his eyes, the way he'd wanted to give her pleasure, not snatch it for himself.

Like Brian had.

Forget Brian.

But she couldn't.

He'd ripped out her ability to trust another man. Had created in her such uncertainty and disbelief in herself that she didn't think anyone could love her.

But she'd thought—hoped—she'd seen a glimmer of something special in Adam's eyes as he'd held her in his arms and stayed wrapped in her all night. She'd woken to find the bed strangely cold and empty, as if Adam had always been there. As if he was meant to be there. And now he was gone.

And in less than a fortnight she'd be gone too. Confusion didn't come close. Her head spun with plans and ideas, all of which involved either her staying or Adam accompanying her on her trip. But that would be so much to ask, of either of them. And what if they weren't meant to be together? What if he wasn't The One? What if the whole thing ended in disaster again?

Her brain bouncing off her skull, she slipped out of bed, shrugged into her dressing gown and went to make coffee. Caffeine: panacea of the confused mind.

'Hey.' Sean's head lifted above the laptop screen on the kitchen table. 'Good night?'

'Yes, thank you.' Skye pursed her lips and hoped her baby brother wouldn't ask any more. In reality she should be cross at him for throwing Adam the key, but how could she be mad after what had happened?

'Decent bloke, that Adam.' Sean stood and flicked the kettle on. 'Coffee?'

'Sorry?' Astounded, she felt her brother's forehead. 'Are you sickening for something?'

'Can't a guy be nice to his sister?'

'Not unless he's had a personality transplant.' As he stuck a hot mug into her hand and grinned, *astonishment* morphed into *frank suspicion*. 'Okay. How much do you want?'

'One-fifty. I'll pay you back. I promise. I get paid next week.' He shuffled a hand through his messy hair and then pointed to the laptop. 'It's for a good cause.'

She peered over his shoulder, determined not to get sucked into another one of her brother's hare-brained ideas. The online poker had proved very costly, as had the lawn-mowing business without a lawnmower. 'So, what's new this week?'

He picked up a brochure next to the laptop and showed her. 'I'm enrolling in a motorcycle course, but you have to pay up front.' Clipped to the shiny brochure was a note in Adam's handwriting. Her heart tripped as she read.

Sean, if you ever get to be half as good as me on a bike you can take my baby for a spin. Do this course and you'll be halfway there. Adam.

She couldn't help smiling. With that note Adam was making a commitment to hang around, let Sean ride his bike, maybe even forge a relationship with her brother. He'd taken on board the fact that her boys needed a good role model and appeared to be stumping up to do the job. Or was she jumping the gun here? But surely Adam wouldn't make such a promise if he didn't intend to fol-low through.

Suddenly, and unbidden, intense sadness shook through her. How dare he whip in here and steal all their hearts? Even if, with Sean, it amounted to pure bribery. But it had worked. And she owed him more than ever. She noticed the *'PTO'* at the bottom. 'Oh, there's more.'

'It's nothing.' Sean flushed and tried to snatch the paper out of her hand.

'Oh, no, you don't.' She dodged out of his way and read the back.

Do not ask your sister for the cash. If you don't have enough I have plenty of jobs you could do to help pay for the course. Get in touch.

A secret smile blossomed in her heart. Seemed he had the measure of her brother altogether. Making Sean work for once. And protecting her. Protection she could do in spades, she'd fought hard battles for her brothers—to ensure they had the best start in life. Had seen them through the desertion of their dad, the death of their mother. Each time feeling the pain evident in their pubescent eyes. Sure, she'd done more protection than the average young woman, but she'd never been protected before. It felt weird, nice. Warm. And made it harder for her to leave by the minute. 'Great one, Adam.'

Sean grimaced. 'I thought it'd be quicker if I asked you.'

'Easier, you mean. Read it again. *"Do not ask your sister for cash."*' She bopped him on the head with the note. He had the decency to look shamefaced. 'Even if Adam hadn't written that, I wouldn't give you the cash. You can go out and earn it, like everyone else.'

Sean looked at her and frowned, more confused than upset. 'You know, you've changed.'

Confidence straightened her back. 'Too right I have.'

He nodded. 'Good. I like it.' Then he rolled his sleeves up. 'I wonder what jobs he had in mind. I'll call him later, once I've tidied up.'

She stared at him open-mouthed. 'What?'

'Tidying? *A place for everything and everything in its place.* What Mum used to say, right? I don't know what all the fuss is about.' He shrugged and cleared the dirty pots from the table. 'It only takes a few minutes and now I can find all my stuff. You were right all along. I guess.'

Her brother cleaning? 'About that personality transplant…'

'And we've been royal pains in the butt? Right?'

'You sure have.' She went to place a kiss on his cheek, but he dodged out of the way. Her brothers never had done the sloppy stuff.

Yeehah! Finally! If Adam had been there she'd have kissed him too, long and hard. They'd created a miracle!

Her stomach clutched tightly, and she realised she wanted to kiss Adam long and hard anyway, regardless of miracles. She wanted to kiss him every day, here, at work. In the waterfall. Flying high in a balloon. In Europe. London. Anywhere. Everywhere.

Everywhere. Whatever happened, she wouldn't cancel her trip. She'd worked too hard to give this up. But maybe he'd consider coming with her. Have a shorter stint abroad, get some work experience and then return to Atanga Bay where he could settle. There had to be an answer that worked for both of them. If he wanted her.

But what if he didn't want her in the end? That clutch around her heart tightened like a vice, the familiar doubt creeping in. He wouldn't want her. He wasn't a for-ever kind of guy. He'd done the marriage thing and had been burnt. Something in his eyes told her he wouldn't be rushing into it again. And definitely not in the next few days.

But that didn't make her want him any less. Didn't erase the image of his gorgeous body wrapped in her sheets.

Didn't mean she couldn't enjoy another night with him. And if her heart got broken in the process, then at least she'd had the courage to let him in. At least she'd known how wonderful love could be.

Love. Yeah. Without a doubt. The realisation hit her full force in her gut. She winced and grabbed the back of a chair. She loved him. *Damn. Why now?*

'Sis, you okay?' Sean's hand on her shoulder jolted her out of her reverie.

'I'm fine. Thanks. Got a few things on my mind.'

'Not long to go, eh? Bet you can't wait to leave all this behind.' He slicked a kiss on her cheek and slouched out the door. 'See ya!'

'No. Can't wait.' *Liar.* She slammed two pieces of bread into the toaster. Love? It was terrifying and wonderful at the same time. Not controlling or manipulative, not filled with lies and broken promises. Not unrequited and innocent. Just simple, respectful, passionate. Hot.

'You fool, Skye Williams. What have you got yourself into this time?' As she spoke she checked the door, to make sure Adam hadn't caught her talking to herself again. And was disappointed not to see him there in his black leathers with sex written across his gaze.

She didn't want it to end. Not right now. She just had to count the hours until she saw him again, try to convince him to take what they had to another level. For as long as they had left. Mutual appreciation, an affair, a fling, a relationship however short-lived. Maybe even broach the idea of him coming with her to Europe, test the waters, see how he might feel about it. Because no matter what the outcome, she couldn't give him up just yet.

Okay, she'd been stupid to let him in, to make that connection deeper, to allow him to take a piece of her heart.

But like a motorbike careering out of control, faster and faster, she had no ability to stop it.

Adam lay on the hard hospital bed and tried a million different ways to text Skye without worrying her. He'd said he'd catch up with her later. Now it was well past later and so many things had happened so quickly he didn't know where to begin.

Don't panic, but...

I'm in hospital, but...

My foot's going to be okay, but...

In reality it changed nothing. Only he'd be cooped up here instead of Atanga Bay, she'd still be organising and packing. Come a week on Thursday she'd be on the plane as planned and he'd just be sitting and waving her off instead of standing. But he'd wanted the next few days together to be special. Instead, he'd be on high-dose analgesics with the contents of a DIY shop affixed to his leg.

Glancing at the 'No Mobile Phones' sign, he tapped in her number. Hell, it was a private room, what harm could he do? 'Skye?'

'Adam? Hi.'

It was a relief to hear her voice. He imagined her pretty face and nose wrinkling as she spoke. He ached to be with her, seeing her bright smile instead of the stark, snot-green walls of this soulless room. He tried for light. 'You won't believe where I am.'

'No?'

'St Paul's Private Hospital. Auckland.'

'Nice, very posh.' He heard the appreciation in her voice. 'Are you transferring a patient?'

'No. I am the patient.'

She gave a sharp intake of breath. 'Your foot?'

He kicked the starched sheets off his legs and looked

down at the mess he'd been hiding from for too long. Much to his chagrin, painkillers and ignoring it hadn't made it go away. But when everything had slotted into place, a home, a job, a girl…he hadn't wanted to spoil it all by an operation and a long recovery. Just to start from scratch again.

'Yes. The doc says he needs to re-fix it and has a free slot tomorrow morning. More plates and screws. I'm like a magnet as it is. I'll have metal things attracted to me as I walk round. Damn thing.'

'Better keep out of the kitchen, then. All that cutlery. I knew you were going to need something done to it. It looked really nasty.' She paused as if letting it all sink in. 'So, what do you need? I can come down now and drop things off. I have work in the morning, but I can finish early—'

'No.'

'No?'

'Skye, stay there. I'm fine.' She couldn't see him like this. Pain he could manage, he'd been trained to deal with it, but letting her see him weak? Never. Knowing Skye, she'd cluck around him too, fussing over a leg he'd have trouble with the rest of his life. He'd got over it but couldn't stand her pity. No amount of feeling sorry for himself would change the fact he'd be lame, less than perfect. *You're not the man I married, Adam.* Better that she stay away. 'I'll be in here for a couple of days, but I have everything I need.'

Apart from you.

He banged a fist against his head. Why torment himself with more what-ifs, the texture of her skin, the colour of her eyes, the tight fit of their bodies together, when there was no future for them? Better just to end it now. He had to let her go. For both their sakes. 'I'll get Dan to pick me up a few things if I need them.'

'Oh. Okay.' She sounded put out. 'What about your job?'

'It's taken a lot of sweet-talking but they've promised to keep it open for me and I have to pass a repeat physical assessment. There's a good six weeks' recovery after the op. And a lot of work ahead.' How many times had this foot been worked on? Four? And it would never be right, but so far he'd managed to suck up the pain. Just. When that helicopter had gone down, man, he'd underestimated the effect it would have on the rest of his life.

'Then I'm going back to work on a part-time basis. The boss has been fantastic so I need to recuperate well and stick to the physio programme. Don't want to let him down.'

'No. I suppose not. Six weeks. Wow.'

They both knew what that meant. He'd be out of action for a long time, way past her leaving and then some. Not that it mattered, he hadn't planned on going with her. Had no plans to set foot on one plane, let alone the number of flights she'd organised, or on taking a chance with someone he'd only really just met, no matter how deeply he felt for her.

He hadn't intended to make love to her, or to stay the night. He never stayed the night. But he'd had no compulsion to leave her, had just wanted to make love to her over and over. To feel her beside him, to pretend they had a lifetime together and not a few days. To be with a woman who made him feel good about himself, a woman who made each day special, bright and fun.

So why the hell did he feel as if his world had been ripped apart?

'Great that he's keeping the job open for you.' She sighed, sounded tired. Dejected. Her voice was flat and lifeless. And it was his fault. 'Well, if you don't need me...'

If only she knew.

'Babe?' He cringed. Babe? *Babe?* Damn it.

Static filled the line. Out in the corridor the dinner trolley clanged, crockery chinked. The world carried on while his had shattered into confused pieces that refused to fit back together. He slammed the door and craned to hear her speak.

When she did she sounded unsure and hesitant. She cleared her throat. 'About last night… Do we need to talk?'

The best night of his life. It happened, it wouldn't happen again. 'There's not a lot to say, is there?'

'I enjoyed it.'

Remembering the oil, he grinned. 'Me too.'

'You want to do it again?'

'Whoa. Skye. We shouldn't get carried away.' That would be stupid. And foolish. But, oh, so good.

'Because you don't want to? Or because it would be very silly at this stage?'

Because he would forget the promises he'd made, because he'd want more of her. Because he was already afraid to let her go. 'The latter. Obviously.'

Silence stretched between them. He dragged the sheets back over his legs. Kicked them off. Stared at the ceiling, the dimpled tiles. The windowless room. Didn't want to say the words that would end this. But felt them there at the back of his throat. Waiting for a decent amount of guts to say goodbye.

Then she whispered, 'Adam?'

'Yes.'

'Are you in a private room?' The whisper deepened, purposeful and charged.

'Yes.'

'No nurses? Auxiliary staff? Patients?'

He didn't know where this was going but he could guess. A jolt of awareness fired into his groin. She wasn't quite the inexperienced innocent he'd pegged her as. As he'd discovered last night. *Thank God.* 'No, it's just me. Why?'

'Last night. Tell me which bit you enjoyed the most.'

'All of it.' He didn't want to be reminded of the exquisite details of what he'd be giving up. But the night replayed over and over in his head like a damned video.

'I want more details than that. Which part? The part when you kissed me and I sucked your tongue deep into my mouth? The part where you nibbled my nipple? The part...'

His body burned for her. 'God, Skye. You're making me want you all over again.'

'That is the general idea. Do you want me, Adam?'

He could stop this right now. But that would be a lie and he would never lie to her. After what Brian had put her through she deserved honesty, even if it got them into deeper trouble. 'Hell, yes.'

'Then make me a promise that as soon as we can, we will repeat last night.'

His gaze rested on a poster on the wall advertising some healthy-heart organisation. *Treat your heart well.*

Too late, mate. 'I can't make promises I can't keep...'

She growled. 'Ruin the moment, why don't you? Don't give me that rubbish about how much time we have left. Can't we make the most of it? Enjoy it for what it is? I want you. You want me. It's basic maths. One plus one.' Her laughter made him press the phone closer to his ear just so he could hear it more clearly. He was going to miss that.

'You make me feel good, Adam. We're two consenting adults who know what we're getting into. When it's time to say goodbye we can end it like adults.'

'Easy to say.'

'We'll be okay. There's no secret agenda. I'm not asking for for ever, just a few days. What do you say? More kissing?'

But he didn't know if he could. If he kept his lips pressed together he wouldn't say something that would get them into deeper trouble.

'Adam? You still there?'

He closed his eyes, as if that would erase the images swirling in his head. The total satisfaction he'd felt being with her. 'Yes. Still here.'

'Good. Now, if you don't give me an answer in two minutes, I'll have to tell you how good you made me feel. Describe what I'm wearing, how hot it is here in my bedroom. How much I want to feel you inside me again.' He heard her swallow deeply, imagined her in that lacy number again. His resolve started to melt. He heard the smile in her voice. 'I can be very persuasive.'

'I don't doubt it.' Man, he wanted Skye more than he'd wanted anyone in his life. And he had a few nights left to spend with her. She was offering a no-strings affair.

Why waste that opportunity? Damn it, he'd hate himself for ever if he didn't take this chance to be with her. 'Okay, Skye. As soon as I get out of here, come round.'

'Good. I can make you feel a lot, lot better.' Her breathing quickened. 'In the meantime, let's talk about my favourite part of the other night.'

The door squeaked open and a nurse came in, carrying a clipboard. She opened her mouth to speak then frowned at the sight of his phone. He nodded and flashed a smile. 'Skye, I have to go, there's someone here.'

'Okay. Good luck, then.'

'Yeah. No worries. Happy packing. See you in a few days.'

'Okay. Adam...' She paused. More static filtered

through the airwaves, along with a deep yearning that only ever seemed to grow more intense. 'You know…'

Everything she didn't say filled the gap between them. He felt it through every cell in his body. Something he didn't want to name. 'Yeah, yes, Skye. I do.'

CHAPTER TWELVE

'I'M TERRIBLY sorry, but Dr Wiseman's clinic's running a little late this afternoon. We had an emergency.' Skye flashed her full-watt beam at Mrs Davis as she steered her towards the waiting room. 'We'll be as quick as we can.'

Glancing at the wall clock, her stomach tightened. Adam had been home for two hours and every atom in her body wanted to run down Main Street and leap into his arms. But, no, a diabetes check, a catch-up MMR vaccination and an immigration medical still kept her from her man.

She shook her head. Not even when she and Brian had been in the first flush of romance had she been so distracted. Her rash attempt at seducing Adam over the phone had put her head in a daze. Three days ago she'd been melted by lust and the shocking realisation that she had fallen in love with the mysterious soldier. Ill timed, ill advised and deeply selfish, but she'd devised a plan that would help Adam both recuperate and allow them to spend their last few precious days together. She just had to get him to agree.

But right now she had a job to do. She glanced at the patient folder in her hand and busied herself. 'Mr Atwell? Would you like to come through?'

Mrs Atwell patted her husband's arm with her liver-spotted hand as the old couple settled into chairs in Skye's consulting room. 'He's not doing the right things. I keep telling him, you have to cut the carbohydrates, but he sneaks lollies when I'm not looking. And he's a terror with the salt and vinegar chippies.'

The old man shrugged, his green woolly jumper riding up his rotund stomach, his feet swelling out of ankle socks and sandals. He didn't look like he could ever be a terror.

Skye didn't have the heart to reprimand him, he'd been attending diabetic clinics for longer than she'd been alive. She made a note for yet another dietician referral and a longer consultation to discuss the basics of diabetes management. Again. Still, he'd reached the ripe age of eighty-six and not done any serious damage so far.

'Well, your blood sugar is a bit higher than I'd like, the tablets can only work so far, but you do have to do your bit. As you know, the secret is not giving in to temptation in the first place. If you don't have sweets in the house, you won't have them wafting under your nose screaming, *Eat me*.'

God knew, good sense told her she needed to follow that advice. If she didn't go near Adam, she wouldn't be tempted. Easy, right? But, like Mr Atwell, she'd never been overly good at self-control. She passed the theory with flying colours, but her practice totally sucked.

The old man's cheeky eyes met hers as he pulled his wife into a bear hug. 'I always think that a bit of what you fancy does you good. That right, Alice?'

Good point. A terror, and wise too.

'Get off with you.' His wife gently pushed him away. The love in her eyes was blatant yet soft. 'He's never been one to do as he's told, not in sixty-nine years of marriage.'

'Sixty-nine years? That's amazing.' Skye watched as they dithered around each other, Mrs Atwell straightening his tie, Mr Atwell pulling the chair out for her to sit. They were two parts of the same well-oiled machine. Two halves of a whole. More than a whole. Her heart softened to watch them. How beautiful to love and be so loved.

'Yes, well, I knew I had to marry her the minute I set eyes on her.'

Mrs Atwell blushed like a teenager and her face transformed, eyes lit with the tender mist of memory. 'We were only seventeen. Met at a Wellsford dance. And he was going away to war in a couple of weeks so we had to make it quick.'

'I needed to snap her up before anyone else had the chance. A beauty like that. I wanted her to have my name in case...well, in case I didn't come back. They were difficult times, nothing was ever certain.'

Skye had often stopped and paid her respects at the Atanga War Memorial. Almost a generation of men wiped out. Mrs Atwell had been lucky to get her husband back. 'But you did come home.'

'I did. Damaged in body, but not in mind.' In answer to Skye's raised eyebrows he continued, 'Got ambushed at a roadblock. Grenades popping like firecrackers. It was touch and go for me for a while. Still got shrapnel in my back. I always say I carry a bit of Italy with me wherever I go.'

'Nasty business, that war, it took some time to get over it all. I was so glad to get him home.' The old lady ran her hand down her husband's spine, her shaking hands pinpointing the place where the shrapnel had hit. Judging by the way her eyes brimmed with tears, Mrs Atwell had been deeply affected by her husband's injury.

For a moment Skye's throat filled with a tight knot, imagining the intense anxiety a wife, mother, sister had felt when their men had left to go to war. The terrible news they'd been injured, or worse, and the unknown state in which they'd return. Skye would bet the old lady had been a constant source of support. And somehow they'd both worked through it and come out whole.

With his loyalty and integrity, not to mention his hidden humour and passion, Adam Miller was just about the most whole man Skye had ever met. His wife must have been a fool to let him go.

But wasn't that the route she planned to take too? Fly off into the sunset, leaving him here with an injury and weeks of physio ahead of him. Her gut twisted as indecision and confusion wrought their way through her brain.

'But after all that she never stopped loving me.' Mr Atwell held his wife's hand now.

'No, I never stopped loving him.'

Forget the diabetes check. Skye just wanted to cry all over them. Sixty-nine years together and they obviously loved each other as much now as they had at the beginning. She managed to swallow the lump and put voice to the question that had been nagging her for the last few days. 'But how did you know after such a short time that this was the person you wanted to spend your life with?'

'I just did.' They spoke at once. Laughed, waited for the other to finish. 'I just knew.'

As if it was the most obvious answer in the world.

But did she know? Skye cranked the handbrake as she pulled up later outside Adam's house. Did she know she wanted to spend the rest of her life with him? And did he? Sure, their lovemaking had been sensational, but to hang a future on it?

Silly girl. Remember Mum. A woman who'd hung her hopes on a man. Provided him with three children and years of devotion. The first time she'd needed something back, he'd disappeared.

Remember *Brian*. Enough said.

She climbed out of the car, balancing a Crockpot in one hand. Adam hadn't offered her a future, he'd offered her his bed. Friendship. A fling. Just about all he could offer given the circumstances. And she was going to grasp it with both hands. The future be damned.

The sound of the door creaking open jerked Adam from his analgesic haze on the sofa. Pressing the lid down on the small jewellery box curled into his palm, he stuffed it under one of the cushions. *No hurry*. He had to pick the right moment.

'Is that you, Skye?' His first thought. Hope. That she'd finally arrived.

'Hey, soldier boy. You okay?' She kissed his forehead. His nose. His scar. Swirls of vanilla filled the room as he pulled her to him. A big pot of something that smelled delicious, wrapped in her hands, worked as an infuriating barrier between them. But his lips found hers and she opened her mouth to welcome him in. Three days apart had felt like three months. He flattened his hands against her back, pressed her closer.

Memories of being deep inside her rolled over him, and it was all he could do to stop himself yanking her clothes off there and then. 'Should we skip dinner and go straight to bed?'

Her fingers tiptoed up his chest. Too much fabric in the way. He slid his fingers under the flimsy silk of her top.

She pulled away. 'Oh, God, I've missed you, Adam. Give me a second to pop this Crockpot down somewhere.' She searched around the room, fixed on the kitchen door. 'I'll be right back, then I can help you get comfortable.'

Comfortable? Comfortable? How could she choose

comfortable over getting hot and steamy? 'I don't want comfortable. I'm not an invalid.'

Was that how she saw him? Someone to comfort? Someone to pity? An invalid? He wouldn't act like one and wouldn't be treated like one. Heat fizzled away.

He swung his leg to the floor and reached for his crutches. 'Let me help. Can I get you a drink? Wine?'

'I brought beer, thought you'd prefer it.' She glanced over to the brown tablet bottles and foil packages on the coffee table. 'Oh, I never thought. You probably shouldn't drink while on those.'

'No.' He needed a clear head anyway. As if that would be possible with the thick fug of codeine messing up his brain. And Skye standing there in front of him, her lips swollen with his kiss and his body remembering promises he wanted her to keep. Right now. Upstairs. His whole body buzzed with need for her.

'Adam. Sit down, I can get everything. Now point me to the kitchen. I'll be right back.' She headed to the kitchen door.

'Through there. But I've got dinner sorted.' As he took a step he buckled to the side. Grabbed for the edge of the sofa. Missed. Landed on his backside on the floor. Pain sheared through his leg. The darned crutches had a mind of their own.

With every ounce of effort he could muster he took his weight on his biceps and levered himself from the floor. Jerk. Fool. *Weak.*

He smashed the foot of the crutches onto the carpet and hopped behind her into the kitchen, hoping she hadn't seen his stupid fall. Caught the look of shock on her face.

But she was staring at the table, not his leg. 'What's all this?'

'Okay, so it's hardly cordon bleu, but I didn't want you

coming round here after a day's work and then having to
cook a meal.'

'But candles? Serviettes? Salad and pizza? Seriously,
you've only just come out of hospital, you shouldn't have.
I want to look after you.'

'That's what bothered me.' He'd had his fill of being
nursed. Wanted Skye to see beyond his injury. Wanted her
to see herself as more than a carer. To put her own needs
above everyone else's. 'The next thing we know you'll be
offering to move in and look after me, then put your trip
on hold and—'

'This casserole can do for tomorrow, then.' She flashed
him a strange look, half hurt, half confusion, then turned
and placed the pot on the counter. For a second her shoulders lifted as she took a deep breath and kept her tensed
back to him.

Goddamn. No. That wasn't her agenda, surely? Moving
in? Giving up her trip?

'Skye?'

She pivoted to face him. 'Would that be such a bad
thing? Me moving in here, or you coming to stay with me,
just for a few days until you're feeling better? I can help
you get around, make sure you're okay. I want to help you.'

'I don't need your help.' The last time he'd been this
damned vulnerable his marriage had crumbled. He didn't
do reruns of his failures.

'Really? You want us to pretend that you didn't just fall
on your ass out there? That everything's fine? That you
haven't had surgery on your foot and you're in a lot of pain?
Sure.' She looked like she wanted to kick the crutches out
from under his armpits. But she sat at the table. 'I'm a
trained health professional, I know how to help.'

'I can manage on my own. I don't need some woman
taking pity on me.'

Her eyes glistened. 'Gee, thanks. There's a ringing endorsement of me and my nursing skills.'

'It's not your nursing skills that are in question.'

She glared at him. 'So what is it?'

'I don't want you to rethink your plans on my account.'

'You think I'm going to throw my life away on you?' She shook her head.

He threw the crutches to the floor and sat opposite her. 'Aren't you? Isn't that what's on your mind?'

'Time spent with you wouldn't be a waste, Adam.'

'You don't think?' He wouldn't be responsible for someone else losing out on their dreams just because of him.

'I have been thinking. Actually. Perhaps I could postpone my tour, just fly direct to London in a few weeks to take up my job.' She folded the serviette into a tiny fan of creases, then unfolded it. Folded it again. Kept her eyes on the process, didn't look at him. 'You could come with me and we could travel in a few months' time, take a holiday.' She sounded like she expected rejection.

'Go with you? To London?' This was worse than he'd feared. He'd been tempted—sorely tempted—to ask her to stay, had even anticipated her suggesting delaying things. But flying out with her? 'Go backpacking around the world with a gammy leg? Give up my job here, everything I'm working towards? Give up my promises?' Get on a goddamned plane?

'I know it's a lot to ask.' She shrugged her shoulders and her expression turned from anxious to dejected. 'It's probably stupid. But think about it?'

'You know I can't do that.'

'Is it the flying thing?'

'No.' Yes. That played a part. But no way would he admit that.

'The ex-wife thing? Losing your friends? I'm trying to understand here why you won't even take a chance.'

'It's all of those things and none of them. I can't explain.' *I'm scared of losing something so beautiful. Scared of holding you back, making you regret things you didn't have, didn't do.* 'I can't come with you, Skye. And there's no way in hell I'm letting you stay here. End of.'

Dark shadows fell over her eyes. She crumpled the napkin into a tiny ball and wrapped her fist around it. Her sunny smile had completely disappeared. He ached to put it back there, but he couldn't make promises he would never keep. Make something up just to make her feel better for a short while.

He wondered if this was how she'd looked when Brian had told her all their plans for a future had been a lie. That he'd never considered giving up his marriage for her. That, to him, she'd been an interesting sideline, a distraction.

Was that how she felt right now too? That he'd been okay with a fling but not with commitment?

She'd probably never understand that his reasons for letting her fly were for her benefit. That he wasn't like Brian.

She wiped the back of her hand across her eyes. 'I suppose everything was fine when you just thought we'd be having a no-strings affair?'

'No.' He cursed under his breath. 'We were fooling ourselves. We're in way deeper than we should be.'

No strings.

Damn it, he wanted strings. He wanted ties that bound. He'd wanted them since the day his parents had gone out on that shopping trip and never returned. Since the social worker had sat him down and told him, at the age of six, that he'd be going to live with another family. And he'd bitten and scratched and kicked his way out of that home, and the next and the next. Because wherever they'd placed him hadn't been where his parents were.

For the rest of his life since then he'd searched and searched for something to love and had ended up losing everything. His family, his wife and his friends. The people he should have saved.

But the kind of strings Skye was talking about—an uncertain future in a distant country—hadn't been part of his plan.

He'd have to conquer more than his fear of flying. If he could even get on a plane. He'd have to find another job. This one had been hard enough to come by and he was holding on by a shred.

And more, he'd have to take the biggest risk of all and put his trust in Skye. Trust her to put herself first regardless of his needs, trust her to love him with all his flaws. Trust her to do everything she wanted to do in her life, with him or without him. Not compromise because his leg couldn't take it. Or because he was tired. He wanted her to do what his friends couldn't; live life without regret.

He'd have to trust her. Period.

But now…? So soon after meeting her? And when he'd got his own future mapped out? He couldn't forget the promises he'd made as his friends had lain dying. That he'd do them proud. And he was halfway to achieving that. Living out his life in sleepy Atanga Bay. Alone. It was more than he deserved for surviving. More than they'd ever have.

'There are too many things against us right now, Skye. In a different time, if we were both in the same space, who knows? Perhaps we could have made a go of it. I'm so sorry…' He put his hand over hers.

She snatched hers back as if she couldn't bear him touching her. But gave him a half-smile. This time it wasn't the one she wore to help others through the day, or the one that told him she was happy. This was the smile that told him her heart was breaking, but she wouldn't let him see it.

'Hey, it's okay. Silly me, getting ahead of myself. Of course you wouldn't want to come.' She threw the crumpled napkin across the table. 'I'd better go. The boys will be wondering where I got to.'

'No. Stay a while.' He couldn't bear to lose her just yet. This time his heart would stay broken in tiny pieces. Because there'd be no Skye to fit it back together again.

Do not cry. Walk away. The tightness in Skye's chest became almost unbearable. For a few seconds there she'd allowed herself to believe in a silly dream where she could have it all. But really? She should have known better. Adam had made his mind up. It wasn't about the distance between them—as a soldier he'd endured much worse.

She knew that he had deep feelings for her, even though he wouldn't admit it. That he'd mixed up pride and loyalty and come up with some strange kind of martyrdom that didn't allow compromise. That he didn't feel worthy of being happy.

Damn it, if she hadn't fallen head over heels for the world's most stubborn man.

She knew too well not to make a scene or a fool of herself. Brian had laughed in her face when she'd confronted him. Her mum had ended up alone when she'd asked for something for herself. Better to keep her true feelings hidden deep—that way there'd be no messy scene or hysterics. Bad enough for him to think she'd be prepared to compromise her plans for him.

The steely look in his eye resembled the one she'd seen that first day. Back to brooding and being stubborn. What she'd learnt of him so far had taught her she wouldn't be able to raise a smile out of him now.

And once he'd determined to do something he'd never change his mind.

No matter how much he hurt. No matter how much he hurt her.

It would only take an inch or so to touch him, to feel his hard chest, run her fingers over the tattoo that gave him pride and sorrow in equal parts. To lose herself in him, the way she'd done that one night. That wonderful night when he'd been the most carefree and she'd glimpsed how he might have been without the ghosts that haunted him still.

And she'd known then how much she'd loved him, would always love him.

Which made everything she did now that much harder.

'I need to go.' She stood and scraped the chair back across the wooden floor. 'I have a lot to do. Packing, mostly.'

'I'd like to see you before you go.' He reached for her but she shrugged him off.

'Maybe.' Her body shook, her hands trembling as she turned the doorhandle.

Then she turned and walked slowly out of the kitchen, through the lounge towards the front door, her back straight, her shoulders hitched, her fists tight by her sides.

Attagirl. Use the anger to fuel your dreams. Go and don't look back.

No way would he allow her to compromise her plans to stay with him.

But that didn't stop him reaching for her. Didn't stop the insatiable need to hold her and pretend they could have a future somehow. Somewhere.

He heard the click as the front door opened. Grappled for his crutches. Half hopped and stumbled. And fell hard against the door.

No. The word screamed in his head. 'Skye…'

But letting her go had to be the best thing for them both.

Every cell in his body ached to haul her back. To proclaim his love for her. Because that's what this felt like. The thing he'd been searching for all his life. He'd found it, when he hadn't been looking, right here with this woman. Ethereal yet substantial. Deep, painful, heart-wrenching yet liberating. *Love*. God, yes. He loved her.

For what use that was. If he loved her then he had to let her go. No matter how painful it was—a damn sight more painful than the ache throbbing through his foot. More painful than watching his wife as she'd packed her things. More painful in some ways than watching his friends die, because even though he carried the guilt of their deaths, he knew he wasn't responsible for them. Knowing he was responsible for Skye's pain now cut to the core.

He limped into the lounge, the roar of her car engine covering the silent scream in his head. Slumping down onto the sofa, his hip hit against something hard. 'Damn.'

He rooted under the cushion, took out the jewellery box and threw it against the goddamned wall.

CHAPTER THIRTEEN

'THE final round is dedicated to our very special guest tonight. We have ten questions about…Skye Williams!' The quizmaster tapped the microphone and demanded quiet. 'Don't worry, Skye, they're not too personal! Question one, what was the name of Skye's first pet dog?'

'Oh, no.' Skye covered her face with her hands and squirmed with embarrassment. Organising her farewell party to coincide with the quiz had been a monumental mistake. She should have done exactly what she'd felt like doing and disappeared without a word. Taken her breaking heart and full backpack on to the next chapter of her life, instead of hiding her sadness from fifty people all insistent she have a good time.

'Give us a clue.' Mim leaned in and whispered, 'I know it's cheating, but we're not doing so well tonight. You're not yourself. Nerves? Excitement? Mind on other things?'

Adam. Love. The future. 'Nerves, I think.'

'You'll have a ball.' Her old friend and colleague touched Skye's shoulder and Skye felt a lump surge in to her throat again. Nerves didn't come close. Second thoughts, last-minute wobbles, confusion. She'd stopped trying to keep up with the thousands of panicky thoughts running through her brain.

Over the years she'd shared many confidences with

Mim, but what difference would it make now? Adam had made it clear they had no future, and she had no desire to make a fool of herself and go and beg, so no amount of dissecting it over a beer was going to help.

She needed to move on. And was doing that tomorrow morning. With a splintered heart and a large hangover if the amount of farewell drinks in front of her was anything to go by.

Mim nudged her. 'Tigger? Roxy?'

'My lips are sealed.'

'Just a teeny clue? Come on…I remember it was a scabby old mongrel, but the name escapes me.'

'I can't.' She smiled to show her friend she was having a good time. To show herself she could still do it. 'And, by the way, I loved that scabby mongrel to death.'

'It's on the tip of my tongue.' Her friend's eyebrows rose. 'A great godmother you're going to be to little Janey, far too honest. Aren't you supposed to teach her how to get away with things, sneak around, shop? And you'll be far too far away.' Mim squeezed her hand. 'But, still, we'll miss you and we love you to bits.'

'Thanks.' Skye swallowed back the lump. Despite her need to leave and find her own place in the world, to explore and to have a little adventure, she knew she was well loved and would be missed. If not by Adam then by everyone else she loved here.

'Love you too.' She scanned the room for anyone else listening or watching her, then whispered, 'Think Dorothy.'

'No idea what you're talking about. Not helpful.' Mim beckoned Sean over and attempted bribery and corruption to tease the name out of him. To no avail.

Staring at the pub door, Skye willed it to open. For Adam to stalk across the room and admit he'd made a mistake. To tell her he loved her and sweep her off her feet.

Fat chance.

In reality that's all Skye could think about. Not leaving or staying or having a whole quiz round dedicated to her. Adam.

Adam. The only thing that prevented sleep. That had made her postpone packing until the last minute. Adam. She was sure they could have made it. Even after such a short time together she'd realised that Mrs Atwell had been right, you just knew. But one-sided love couldn't matter in the end, he'd made his stance very clear.

But he could at least have come to say goodbye.

'Question two.'

When will this be over?

She twirled her wine glass round on the beermat and cringed at what the next question might be. Blood rushed to her face. All eyes homed in on her. The room began to close in. She'd always hated being the centre of attention, this was way too far out of her comfort zone.

These people knew her so well they'd managed to make up ten questions about her life. No one knew her in Asia or Europe. She had tentative contacts in London, but no friends. Her new-found inner strength—the strength that Adam had seen and coaxed out of her—faltered. The enormity of what she'd planned overwhelmed her. She'd be leaving this place, her home. Everything she'd ever known. To do what? Fulfil a childish dream? What if it didn't work out? What if she hated every single step? Anxiety gripped her stomach.

Her shoulders began to shake. Tears threatened. She was lost and embarking on a journey on her own. Completely alone. After everything she'd been through, the strength she'd garnered through looking after her mum, bringing up the boys, surviving Brian. And now Adam. She didn't know if she had enough strength to leave.

'What was the first CD Skye ever bought? Was it a) *Spice* by the Spice Girls? b) Peter Andre's…?'

It didn't matter. Her hands shook as she raised her glass to take a quick drink. 'Think I'll just get some air.'

Mim's concern made her feel even worse. 'Are you okay? You're very red.'

'It's a bit hot.' Her heart hammered. 'Last-minute jitters. I'll be fine in a sec. I just need air.'

She made it to the door, waving and smiling to everyone as she squeezed past.

But when the cool breeze hit her face she sagged against the wall and let the tears roll.

'Skye?'

'Adam?' He'd come. Her heart ached with happiness and a profound sadness that chilled her. Of course he'd come. Adam was honourable and kept his promises. He never told lies or pretended. His frankness might be brutal at times, but she could rely on him to be honest.

As she opened her eyes she saw his cast, a pair of crutches. His jeans, leather jacket. His beautiful hewn face. She stood up and brushed a hand over her cheeks, certain that her mascara had run. *Great*. His enduring memory of her was going to be that she resembled a panda. 'You came.'

'Of course. Didn't think I was going to let you go without saying goodbye?'

'But I haven't heard anything from you for days.'

He tipped her chin up to look at her. 'I had to give you time to do the things you needed to do. You don't want me holding you back.'

No, he hadn't come to beg her to stay.

Small wonder, and misguided hope. The ache in her heart grew through her chest, spread to her shoulders and burned into her head. Tears filled her eyes, but she blinked them away. Of course he wasn't going to ask her to stay. 'No. I guess not.'

She bit her bottom lip to stem the wobble. She'd perfected the art of pretending she was okay, of that damned stiff upper lip, the plastered-on big-hearted smile. But with Adam's fingers touching her skin she wanted to melt into his arms and cry the night away.

'You want to tell me what all this is about?' He ran his arm down her shoulder and steered her to a picnic table in the pub garden. While everyone inside answered questions about her life, she faced the most difficult one right here.

'I'm scared.'

'Of branching out? Taking a risk?' His eyes filled with concern. 'You are the most amazing person I've ever met. You'll be fine. More than fine. The whole world is out there waiting for you to grasp it by the ball—'

'Horns?'

'Yeah, horns.' He winked. 'You'll meet amazing people, and some not so amazing. You'll visit all those fabulous places. You'll be free, Skye. For the first time in your life. Grasp it.'

Free? Not with the ties binding her to Adam. She'd never be free. She didn't want to be free. 'I don't know if I want to.'

'Of course you do.' His eyes traced the tears running down her cheeks and he gave her a soft smile. He'd come a long way. Smiles came easier to him now, his face had finally perfected the art. 'Hey. You'll do great.'

He thought all this was about her travelling. The truth nagged at her. She had to be totally honest and open her heart to him. Just once, to say it. To lay herself in front of him. To see if he felt the same. Otherwise she'd forever regret not saying the words.

'I'm scared because somewhere along the line I've fallen in love with you, Adam. And I don't know where that leaves us or what you want to do with it.' She shuddered an in-breath, her ribcage shaking with the effort of controlling her breathing. 'But I needed to say it.'

'Thank you.' He wiped her tears away with his thumb, then enveloped her in his jacket. She hugged him feeling his heat, his smell wrap round her. 'That's great, beautiful girl. And sad, too. Very sad. I'm deeply honoured that someone like you should say that to someone like me.'

But he didn't say *I love you too*. Although she didn't expect him to. He didn't ask her to stay, didn't volunteer to go with her. Just left her words hanging in the cool night air.

He reached into his jacket pocket and drew out a box. 'I have something for you. To remember me by.'

No. No. No. She wanted to be with him. She didn't want to remember him.

As if she'd ever forget him. His face and touch were imprinted on her heart like a brand. Despite the things he didn't say, she knew she belonged to him and he to her. But there'd be no convincing him. Stubborn, stubborn man. 'For me?'

'For you.'

'But I don't have anything to give you in return.'

'Oh, Skye, you've given me everything.' He pressed a small black box into her hand, a tad scuffed at the edges but warm from his pocket.

'What is it?' When she opened it she inhaled sharply. 'Oh. My…'

Words tangled with the sobs coming from her throat.

A beautiful silver dragonfly hung from a solid chain.

Tiny pink crystals highlighted its body and wings. So delicate and fragile, like the hope in her heart.

But the message behind it wasn't lost. He thought enough of her to want her to be part of his band of brothers... No... What he'd had with those guys had been so much more. The family he'd spent his life looking for. The family he'd loved. And lost. He was telling her how much he cared for her, how much he was prepared to lose. For her sake.

All hope shattered. This was the end.

Live in the moment, and have no regrets. 'It's the most beautiful thing I've ever seen.'

He took the chain and fastened it round her aching throat. 'So are you, Skye Williams. I'll never forget you. Go and live your life. I look forward to hearing great things. I'll expect nothing less.'

Panic gripped her heart. She couldn't leave him. 'I don't want to go.'

'Of course you do. Give me one of your fabulous smiles.'

Her mouth wouldn't do as it was told. She tried to smile, but couldn't. Couldn't pretend any more. She loved him too much.

Then his lips were on hers, filling her with his taste, pressing against her as if his whole life depended on it. Fire burned through her, mingling with the ice-cold reality of leaving him. But she held him close, committing his taste to memory. His touch, the way her body reacted to him on every level. The way no man would ever make her feel again.

And what he didn't say in words he told her in that kiss. She didn't hear it, but she felt it resonate through every cell.

I love you, he said.

And goodbye.

Six weeks later

'She rides like a dream.'

'She sure does.' Adam slapped Sean on his leather-clad shoulder. After a six-week intensive course the lad had earned the right to take a ride. Even though Adam's heart had been in his mouth for the whole twenty minutes his Harley had been out of his sight. 'You did well on the whole. Took this corner a bit too sharply...'

'But I straightened up, I knew I'd done it wrong and I fixed it.'

'Yes, you did.' Adam flexed his left ankle, free finally from the cast. His body itched to get on that bike and kick free, but his bones hadn't quite healed enough to take control of such a big bike. 'You think you're ready for a passenger?'

'Really? You sure?' Sean grinned. 'Cheers, bro.'

'Okay, one turn round the town then we're done. After this you get those lazy brothers of yours to finish that list of chores I gave you. Okay?' He knuckled the kid's fist. 'Or you don't get another go on this sweet baby.'

'Sure thing. Hop on...' He ducked out of the way. 'Hoppalong.'

'Watch it.' Adam climbed on the back, relished the roar and the jolt as they eased onto the highway. The autumn wind, tinged with sea and the coming winter, whipped against his face. With the buzz and the freedom to be on the open road his spirit soared for the first time since Skye had left.

Until now he'd seen little but blackness, a dark hole with nothing at the end of it. Nothing to hope for, except a life. A job. A home. That would be good enough for some, but he needed more. He needed Skye. With every atom in his

body he knew he loved her and like some crazed martyr
had let her go.

'Whoa. Steady.' He bit the words back. Sean knew the
road, the corners and, most of all, the dangers.

The boys had come a long way with a bit of nudging
and a lot of coercion. Typical lads, left everything to the
last minute. God knew how Skye had put up with them for
so long. But they were good kids really. Just needed direc-
tion. Sean had grasped the mantle, and shown he could
lead once he knew how.

And visiting the Williamses' house had given Adam
a tie to Skye. He heard snippets of her trip, saw the postcards with her neat cursive writing.

To be honest, that had been the main reason he'd started
going round there. To be in the place she'd grown up, to
have some connection with her. The relationship with the
boys had grown out of that. He hadn't ever contemplated
being a father figure, but army training had taught him
how to do that role-model stuff. At least he'd be able to
look her in the eye and say he'd helped her out.

God. He gripped the bike tighter. He wanted to look her
in the eye. More than anything, to hold her, to laugh with
her. To be deep inside her.

What a monumental mistake he'd made. But he didn't
even know where she was, where she was headed. Only
that she had a job somewhere at some point.

They buzzed along the coastal road back towards town,
faster and faster until nothing but blurred images whizzed
by, and even though he knew it was reckless and foolish
he silently willed Sean to drive the bike harder, to obliv-
ion. But nothing would heat the ache in his bones at how
much he'd lost. How he'd been too afraid of everything to
trust his gut. Too afraid of flying. Of trusting, of loving
again. Too afraid of living a good life.

As they drove through town he glimpsed the war memorial up ahead. He tapped Sean. 'Pull up, mate.'

The names of the fallen covered all four sides of the marble statue. As always, Adam's heart pinched at the memory of what he'd seen.

They died that we might live. Sure.

His hand crept, almost instinctively, to his tattoo. *No regrets. Live in the moment.*

The words played over and over in his head like a mixed-up soundtrack. No regrets. Live in the moment. They died…might live. Live in… The only clear word: live.

He'd made Skye go on her journey and live her life. Hiding behind fear and grief and giving up the most beautiful woman he'd ever known in the process. She'd taken him from the shell he'd become to a man who wanted to live. Who wanted to…yeah, okay…smile. She'd opened his heart and shown him how to let love in. And then when offered a chance he'd chosen the safest path.

But this wasn't living, this was existing. What honour would he do his friends if he didn't live a full life? Have a wife and kids? Have Skye? What honour was he doing Skye if he didn't admit truly how much he loved her?

He rested his hand against the monument, felt the carved names beneath his fingers. *That we might live.*

Sean was looking at him with a strange expression. 'You okay?'

'Sure. Hey, listen, do you have a copy of Skye's itinerary?'

The kid scrunched his shoulders. 'Her what?'

'Her trip, where she's going and when?' Suddenly, knowing the details of her trip became imperative. 'Quick.'

'Yeah. Of course, she's my sis—'

'You want to show it to me?'

'Er…she told me not to.'

'And do you always do what your sister tells you?'

Sean grinned. His smile was just like his sister's. Not as bright or as full but just as mischievous. 'But you told me—'

'Okay, okay. Just once you can break a rule. Live a little. And while we're at it…' He stroked his beloved motorbike. Ran his fingers over the leather seat, the shiny chrome. This was going to be harder than he'd thought. But leaving her behind faded into nothing compared with seeing Skye again. If only the flying would be so easy to deal with. 'You fancy looking after my baby for me? I'm going away for a while.'

'Built on the remains of the fourth-century cathedral of Santa Reparata, Florence's Duomo was designed in 1296 by Arnolfo di Cambio—'

'That's enough of that.' Skye flicked the switch on the nasal visitor commentary and took in the relative silence of the huge chasm in which she stood. Whispered voices reached her, but nothing detracted from the amazing richly coloured fresco. Centuries of visitors and pilgrims had worn away the stone flags under her feet. She craned her neck to look up at the delicately painted angels and virtues, and wished for the millionth time she had someone to share this with.

The Asian tour had been wonderful, action packed with activities to take her mind off Adam and the deep yearning she'd had to hotfoot it back to Atanga Bay. But travelling the length of Europe on her own had left her lonely. Sure, she'd met a few single travellers like her, shared evenings on Greek islands, in late-night bars. And it had been wonderful.

And yet…something fundamental was missing. She should be happy to be fulfilling her dreams, but her heart ached, her feet hurt and the beauty of everything she saw seemed tarnished a little by her ennui.

She didn't need to guess why. But she knew she had to do something about it. For six weeks she'd controlled her need to contact Adam, but now the longing to speak to him had become overwhelming. Every night and every morning his image, his kisses, their lovemaking, filled her head. The joy he'd brought to her life. And the sorrow.

She missed him. A deep ache that dogged everything she did, coloured everything she saw. Life would never be the same. Always just a little tarnished without him there.

As she left the Duomo and wandered through the busy streets towards her backpackers she decided she'd phone him that night and tell him how she felt. One last time. Stop him from railroading her into what he thought was good for her and tell him what she wanted. For them both. Which was…what? She didn't know. But anything would be better than this half-existence she'd created.

If Adam had taught her anything it was that she was her own person, who deserved to be treated honestly. And he hadn't been honest with her, not in the true sense. He'd told her what he didn't want and couldn't have. But hadn't told her what he wanted. Or how he felt about her. And if she was going to move on she needed to know. One phone call. To ask if he loved her. To determine the next chapter of her life. And if he denied his feelings for her then she'd go on living. Battered a little and bruised but whole.

The carousel music in the piazza had started to drive him mad.

Adam had sat in the same seat for four hours, staring at every single woman that walked past. If Skye didn't turn up soon he'd get arrested for loitering and showing signs of insanity due to the relentless refrain infiltrating his brain.

Wait. He willed his irritation away. The sun shone through scant white clouds, people around him smiled and nodded. He was in Italy, for God's sake. He'd flown here. Flown. In a plane. Thousands of feet in the air. Okay, so he'd almost taken the horse tranquilisers Connor had given him…but still. He'd done it and survived.

He had a lifetime to wait. A lifetime to spend with Skye. He could wait a few more minutes. Hours. Days, if that's what it took.

He licked more of his gelato and studied her itinerary again. In the haze of packing and dealing with his flying worries maybe he'd got the wrong piazza. Wrong damned country.

No. Ostello Santa Maria, off the Piazza della Repubblica. If he'd checked the name once he'd checked it a hundred times.

Suddenly the hairs on the back of his head stood up, his heart picked up a pace and he knew. Just knew she was standing behind him.

'Adam? Adam? Is that you?'

He pivoted to face her. 'Skye. Thank God.' Just to see her face in the crowd of strangers made his heart sing. Her black spikes and the jewel in her nose and the heavily rimmed eyes, the black clothes. *God*, she was beautiful.

He smiled.

He could do that now. Thanks to Skye and the magic she'd woven around him.

He reached for her but she stepped away.

'What are you doing here?' Confusion and joy meshed in her features but she kept her distance. He'd hurt her and she didn't trust that he was there.

'Aw, I didn't like the chapter I was in so I wrote myself a new one. This is much better. In Italy. Eating gelato.' He offered it to her. 'You want a lick? Espresso. The best.'

'I don't think I could swallow anything right now.' The necklace he'd given her hung around her throat, sparkling in the late-afternoon light. She held the dragonfly pendant in her fist, took it to her mouth and pressed it against her lips. A single tear rolled down her cheek. 'How's your foot? How was the flight?'

'What? Fine.' He didn't want to think about his foot. And definitely needed to forget the twenty hours of hell he'd endured. The panic, the sweat and the abject fear. But he'd arrived in one piece and now it was time to take what he needed. 'Skye—'

'Why are you here? Is this for real?'

He finished the gelato and stood, tried not to limp as he walked to her. Didn't want her to see anything but the man he was, as whole as he could be, and asking her the most important question in the world. 'Thought you might like to come for a ride.'

'A what?' It was her turn to smile. He closed his eyes and thanked every god he knew of and the ones he didn't. He'd managed to put that smile back on her face.

'A ride?' With scorn and not a little embarrassment he indicated the eggshell-blue tinpot scooter he'd hired. 'Don't you dare laugh. It's all they had at such short notice. It's a hairdrier on wheels.'

Her gaze scanned the scooter, then him. Her eyes burning with something he needed to deal with…and very soon. 'It's kind of cute. But so not you.'

'I thought it was more your style.' He reached for her. Again. This time she took a step towards him. Almost… 'So…'

'Oh, no. No, you don't.' She dropped the guidebook she'd been carrying and held up her palms. 'You're not going to—?'

'Kidnap you again? Sure am.' Then he lifted her into his

arms, tasted her mouth. The taste he'd been dreaming of for weeks. Ran his hands down her body, relished the feel of her pressed tight against him. Her hair tickling his nose, her vanilla scent mingling with the espresso. Relished the heat of her skin and the promise in her eyes. Finally, after a lifetime of looking, he'd found exactly where he belonged. Right here, anywhere, with Skye.

He lowered her onto the seat. 'You okay with this?'

'That depends. I need you to be honest.'

He took her hand and held it against his chest. Over his heart. Over his tattoo. *Live in the moment.* 'I love you, Skye. I don't care where you are or what you do, I just want to be with you every step of the way.'

Skye's heart filled with happiness. Adam had given up everything for her and asked for nothing in return. It was more than she'd ever dreamed of. It was everything she'd ever hoped for. 'But what about your job? Your promises?'

'I can get another job. I have good skills, I'm needed. We'll work it out.'

He fixed a helmet on her head and she couldn't help squeezing her cheek against his hand. He stroked her face, love for her blazing in his eyes. 'And I reckon my boys would be damned proud that I'm living again. Don't you?'

'They couldn't be prouder.' She nuzzled against him, remembered the brooding shell of the man she'd met. The depths of sorrow in his eyes then and the joy she saw now. She hugged her arms tight around his waist, laid her head against the solid wall of his back. Of all the places she wanted to go, this was where she felt right at home. Right here, in his arms. 'Where are we going?'

'Paris, London, Barcelona. Anywhere, everywhere. I'm with you every step of the way. But…' He winked. 'First stop. Bed.'

Fourteen months later...postcard from Barcelona

Hey, Boys!
Guess what? Adam and I tied the knot! I know, crazy! We're honeymooning in Spain (as you can see) for two weeks, then cruising through the Med. We have news...might need to sell the Harley and buy a car. Yes! You're going to be uncles. Think of some names for us? Planning a trip back home as soon as Adam can get more leave from his Very Important Ambulance Service advisory job.
Lots of love
Skye, Adam and The Bump xx

* * * * *

A sneaky peek at next month...

Medical Romance™

CAPTIVATING MEDICAL DRAMA—WITH HEART

My wish list for next month's titles...

In stores from 7th December 2012:

- ☐ From Christmas to Eternity – Caroline Anderson
- & Her Little Spanish Secret – Laura Iding
- ☐ Christmas with Dr Delicious – Sue MacKay
- & One Night That Changed Everything – Tina Beckett
- ☐ Christmas Where She Belongs – Meredith Webber
- & His Bride in Paradise – Joanna Neil

Available at WHSmith, Tesco, Asda, Eason, Amazon and Apple

Just can't wait?

Visit us Online

You can buy our books online a month before they hit the shops! **www.millsandboon.co.uk**

1112/03

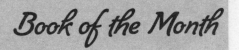

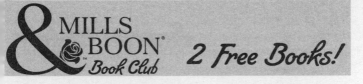

MILLS & BOON® Book Club

2 Free Books!

Get your free books now at
www.millsandboon.co.uk/freebookoffer

Or fill in the form below and post it back to us

THE MILLS & BOON® BOOK CLUB™—HERE'S HOW IT WORKS: Accepting your free books places you under no obligation to buy anything. You may keep the books and return the despatch note marked 'Cancel'. If we do not hear from you, about a month later we'll send you 5 brand-new stories from the Medical™ series, including two 2-in-1 books priced at £5.49 each and a single book priced at £3.49*. There is no extra charge for post and packaging. You may cancel at any time, otherwise we will send you 5 stories a month which you may purchase or return to us—the choice is yours. *Terms and prices subject to change without notice. Offer valid in UK only. Applicants must be 18 or over. Offer expires 31st January 2013. **For full terms and conditions, please go to www.millsandboon.co.uk/freebookoffer**

Mrs/Miss/Ms/Mr (please circle)
_____

First Name
_____

Surname
_____

Address
_____

_____

_____ Postcode _____

E-mail
_____

Send this completed page to: Mills & Boon Book Club, Free Book Offer, FREEPOST NAT 10298, Richmond, Surrey, TW9 1BR

Find out more at
www.millsandboon.co.uk/freebookoffer

Visit us Online

0712/M2YEA

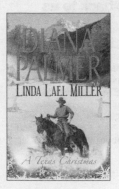

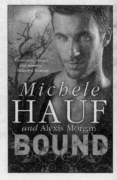

C   JH

Have Your Say

You've just finished your book.
So what did you think?

We'd love to hear your thoughts on our
'Have your say' online panel
www.millsandboon.co.uk/haveyoursay

- Easy to use
- Short questionnaire
- Chance to win Mills & Boon®
  goodies